Alex's face had gone ashen. 'For a moment I forgot who you were. I thought you were...'

'It was bound to happen,' Ginny said swiftly, not wanting him to finish.

'Was it?' He pulled his hand free and doubled it into a tightly controlled fist, his jaw tightening. 'I'm not sure this is such a good idea, Ginny. Seeing you, being with you, especially in this house; it brings Venetia back into my mind all the time.'

Sudden fear gripped her heart, but Ginny managed to say, 'That's inevitable, I suppose.'

'But it isn't fair on either of us,' Alex burst out. 'Especially on you.'

The first half of this compelling story
by SALLY WENTWORTH

TWIN TORMENT

Ginny and Venetia were twins. They looked alike, they thought alike, and all their lives they had shared everything, including their modelling career. Each was the other's best friend—until they both fell in love with Alex Warwick—and life suddenly became a battleground . . .

GHOST OF
THE PAST

BY

SALLY WENTWORTH

MILLS & BOON LIMITED
ETON HOUSE   18-24 PARADISE ROAD
RICHMOND   SURREY   TW9 1SR

First published in Great Britain 1991
by Mills & Boon Limited

© Sally Wentworth 1991

Australian copyright 1991
Philippine copyright 1991
This edition 1991

ISBN 0 263 77291 8

Set in Times Roman 10½ on 12 pt.
01-9111-51497 C

Made and printed in Great Britain

CHAPTER ONE

To see your dead wife walking along the churchyard path towards you had to be a shock for any man. It was for Alex. His face blanched and his body beneath the black overcoat grew rigid. But then he realised who it was, and she saw his shoulders sag in relief. Or perhaps relief was the wrong word. Perhaps it was disappointment. Did he wish her dead and his wife alive?

'Ginny!' Her mother saw her and rushed forward to meet her.

The two women embraced, Ginny's nostrils full of the perfume her mother had always used, a floral, springlike scent that was all wrong now that her mother was middle-aged.

'I'm so pleased you managed to get here. Your father would have been pleased, too.'

As Ginny hadn't seen her father for over ten years, she didn't think that he would have cared much either way. He had another family now, a family that took first place at his funeral and were waiting in a sad group for the coffin to be taken from the hearse. Ginny looked at them, then almost reluctantly turned her head to look at Alex. She hadn't expected him to be here. She hadn't wanted to see him again. It was over five years since they'd last met—and parted, but the circumstances hadn't been blunted by time.

'Hello, Alex.' She tried to say it evenly, but the words came out as cool and withdrawn.

He gave a curt nod in return and deliberately turned his back on her as he offered her mother his arm. 'It looks as if they're going in.'

As her father's eldest surviving child, Ginny should have taken her place in the front pew, but she chose to stand beside her mother during the service. Alex stood on her mother's far side and held a hymn book for her as she dabbed at her eyes with a lace handkerchief. Ginny's parents had been divorced for over sixteen years but her mother still cried for her ex-husband. Ginny had done her crying when she'd first heard the news of her father's death, and she stood dry-eyed, a tall, very slim figure in black.

Her father was to be buried in the village where his family had lived for generations and where he had been brought up. It was the village where he had brought his first wife to live in the family house, so Ginny and Venetia had also been brought up there, until they were ten years old and their parents had separated. Then they had gone to live with their mother. But Venetia, when she had died so tragically, had been laid to rest here in this quiet churchyard, beneath the dark yew trees. Ginny hadn't come to that funeral. But as she stood in the old stone church she became aware of what it must have been like, the sorrow at a young life cut off, and the deep, searing pain of loss and grief of those who had loved her sister. It was almost as if the stones of the walls had absorbed the sadness and held it still. As Alex must hold it still. Ginny stole a glance at him over her mother's head. His profile was a set mask, like a head on a coin, displaying only an outline with no hint at the turmoil of emotions that must lie within.

John Barclay was buried in the family plot, near his ancestors. It was done decently, without haste, although the wind was raw on this April morning. His widow came up to them afterwards. 'You will come back to the house, won't you?'

The mourners began to move away but Ginny hung back. When she was alone she walked the few yards to another grave, its simple stone still comparatively white and new.

Venetia Warwick, daughter of John and Maureen Barclay and dearly beloved wife of Alex. Died, aged 24, together with her unborn child.

Ginny stood looking down at the grave, trying to come close to her sister, but her spirit was no longer here. Ginny had felt it often, and very strongly at first, almost as if Venetia were beside her, as close as they had been together in the womb, but gradually, and to Ginny's deep sorrow, her sister had gradually left her to be alone.

Ginny wasn't much good at praying, and from her own experience had come to doubt whether there was any point in it anyway, but here in this peaceful place, even more than in the church, it seemed the right thing to do. 'Please take care of my sister. Let her rest in peace.' She whispered the words, felt them blow away on the wind. After a moment, Ginny opened her bag and took out a single yellow rose, carefully protected in a cellophane box. Venetia had always liked yellow, and roses had been her favourite flower. Taking it from its wrapping, Ginny bent to lay the flower at the base of the headstone.

There was the sound of an exclamation behind her and the next moment the rose was wrenched from her hand. Startled, she quickly straightened up and found herself looking into Alex's furious eyes. With a gesture of sheer hatred, he flung the rose from him with all the strength of his arm. It flew across the graveyard and landed on a pile of rotting grass cuttings and weeds. An unexpected bonus of degradation.

'Keep away from here,' Alex spat at her. 'Don't you dare sully her grave with your contemptuous offering. You couldn't be bothered to even come to her funeral.'

Ginny stared at him in dismayed alarm, taken aback by his display of anger and resentment. 'I was ill,' she said defensively.

He gave a scornful laugh. 'Too damn caught up in your career, you mean. When I rang your agency in New York to find out what was wrong with you they told me you were away on an assignment.'

It was what Ginny had instructed them to say, not wanting to be disturbed in her grief, but there didn't seem to be much point in telling Alex that. 'I didn't expect *you* to phone me there. Why didn't you call my home number?'

'I did, but I got a permanent engaged signal.' He took an angry step away from her, as if he couldn't bear to be near her. 'What the hell's the point of talking to you? Just get away from here. We don't need you.'

We? Did he still think of himself as part of his dead wife, then? It was almost two years since Venetia had been killed in a horrific car crash on a foggy highway, and Ginny thought that Alex would have started to make a new life for himself by now. But apparently he still grieved inwardly, grieved as much as Ginny did. Today, coming back to the same church, must be an especially difficult time for him. Ginny turned to take a last look at her twin sister's grave, but Alex put an impatient hand on her arm and pulled her roughly away.

'All right, I'm going.' She shook free from his hold, trying to keep her fist clenched, but a drop of blood flew on to his coat.

Alex stared, then caught at her hand, forcing it open when she resisted him. A thorn from the rose had torn a deep scratch across her palm when he had wrenched it from her. The skin around his mouth whitened a little and Ginny guessed that since the accident any sight of a wound must bring memories flooding back. 'Why didn't you say?' he said harshly.

'It doesn't matter.' Ginny tried to take her hand away but he held it firmly.

'Here.' He took a clean handkerchief from an inner pocket and shook it open. 'Use this as a bandage.'

She wrapped it round her hand and tried to tie the ends but it was difficult with one hand. With a smothered exclamation Alex took the handkerchief from her, quickly bound her hand and tied it off neatly. It had taken only a few moments and Ginny had kept her head lowered while he did it, but feeling the strength and warmth of his hand brought so many memories flooding back. Mostly, of course, of that one night they had spent together so many long years ago. A night she had held close to her heart ever since. Her hand trembled a little and Alex gave her a sharp glance. Perhaps he remembered, too, but for him the memory was very different. As soon as the knot was tied, he dropped her hand as if she disgusted him.

His gesture brought back her pride. With a cool, 'Thank you,' Ginny raised her chin and strode away, her walk the long-legged graceful gait of an experienced model.

Most of the other mourners had left, but Ginny's mother was standing talking to some old neighbours that she knew from her time in the village. Ginny had to be recalled to their memory, not that it was really necessary; they all knew that she was Venetia's twin. They offered her their sympathy at the same time as they gave her looks of surreptitious curiosity. It was something that Ginny had become used to in the years that she had become well-known, first as a model and then by the ambiguous term of 'personality'.

'Are you going back to the house?' Ginny asked her mother when the other people moved away.

'Oh, yes, I think so. I won't stay too long, but I'd like to see some of my old friends again.'

'Shall we walk? Most of the people seem to be. Or I've got a car, if you like.'

'I'll walk,' her mother decided. 'I want to see if the village has changed.' She glanced round. 'Where's Alex?'

'With Venetia,' Ginny answered levelly.

Her mother gave her a shrewd glance. 'He was very angry when you didn't come to poor Venetia's funeral.'

'He still is.'

They began to walk down the church path and under the lych-gate into the village street, joining the casual crocodile of mourners, in twos and small groups. The wind was behind them and Maureen Barclay put up her coat collar. 'I'm sure this fake fur you sent me isn't as warm as the real thing. Why did "fur coat" have to become a dirty word just as I was in a position to own one?'

Ginny smiled. 'You wouldn't want animal rights people to shout abuse or throw paint over you, now, would you?'

'Good heavens! Is that what they do in America?'

'It has been known, and in most countries in the world.'

They went on talking at random, but carefully keeping clear of subjects that were likely to hurt, until Mrs Barclay reached out to take Ginny's hand and said, 'I'm really glad you came today. What have you done to your hand?'

'Tore it on a prickly temper,' Ginny said facetiously.

'Alex's, I suppose. You'd never think to see him, so strong and calm, that he could feel such deep and violent emotions, would you? I've never seen anyone so distressed as he was after Venetia was killed. And it was especially bad because of the child. They'd been so looking forward to it's being born. Not that Alex showed his feelings openly for long; after a day or so he bottled it all up inside, you know.' She sighed. 'I think that was worse, really. I'm sure he isn't over it yet.'

Ginny, too, was sure. Because she had loved Venetia as much, if not more, than Alex, and she missed her sister with an aching loss that was almost unbearable every day of her life.

'Where's he working now?' she asked.

'He's at Bristol University, doing some sort of research work. That friend of his, Jeff Ferguson, is there too now. I thought I wrote and told you.'

'Mother, you know you're hopeless at writing letters. All I ever get from you is a postcard when

you're on holiday and Christmas and birthday cards—
and not even those since Venetia died.'

'It seems wrong, somehow, to wish you a happy
birthday when it was Venetia's birthday, too.'

'It's all right, I understand. And you did make the
occasional phone call.'

'But you never asked about Alex and Venetia. I
always wondered what had happened between you and
Venetia to make you go away and cut yourself off so
completely. You had always been so close, all your
lives.' There was an inquisitive note in her mother's
voice but Ginny didn't respond to it. Her tone hard-
ening, Maureen Barclay said, 'Whatever had happened between you, I can't understand your not
coming to Venetia's funeral. I know there wasn't time
for you to get here before she died, but you'd think,
your identical twin sister...'

'I was ill,' Ginny said for the second time that day.

'You're never ill,' her mother said accusingly. 'Why,
it was Venetia who had appendicitis and you didn't.
And she——'

'Do we have to talk about this now?' Ginny cut in
swiftly. 'We ought to be thinking of Dad today.'

Mrs Barclay gave her a mulish look but glanced
round and said, 'Alex is coming. He had some flowers
in the car to put on Venetia's grave.'

He didn't catch them up, although they weren't
hurrying, and Ginny and her mother went into the
house among the other mourners. As soon as she
could, Ginny got hold of one of her aunts, her father's
sister, and asked for the first-aid box. Pleased to have
her to fuss over, her aunt cleaned the scratch and
found a large piece of Band-Aid for her hand. She
even washed the blood off Alex's handkerchief. 'I'll

pop it into a polythene bag for you, shall I? Whose is it?'

'Someone lent it to me. I'll give it back to him.' Ginny took the handkerchief and carefully folded it, before putting it in the bag, realising that she had no intention of returning it to Alex, not now, at least.

When she went back to the room where everyone was gathered, Alex was standing a little apart, an outsider, hardly knowing anyone, a glass of what looked like gin and tonic in his hand. As she entered there was a little silence; that was another thing that Ginny was becoming used to as a minor celebrity, although she was far better known in America than she was in England. Of course, here in this village she was thought of as a local girl made good. But her being successful showed in her clothes and in her poise and self-confidence, all of which attracted curious eyes.

Going over to her father's widow, Ginny offered her condolences and was given a rather cool look in reply. The second Mrs Barclay had never encouraged her husband to keep in touch with his daughters by his first marriage and the girls had seldom been back to the house since their parents had parted. He had, however, given Venetia away at her wedding, which had helped to make up for Ginny's not being there to be a bridesmaid. That people were avidly curious to know why she hadn't been at her sister's wedding Ginny knew, but there was no way she was going to enlighten them. That was a secret between Venetia and herself, and not even her mother knew the reason. Although Alex did, of course. But he was the last person who would ever talk about it.

Her half-sister and -brother, who were in their teens, were standing near their mother. Ginny said hello to them and tried to start a conversation but they were too over-awed, either by her or by the occasion, and Ginny got nowhere with them. With her father's two sisters, though, she had no trouble. 'Your father was so proud of your success in America,' one of them told her. 'He kept all the Press cuttings about you and used to show them to everyone who came round. It didn't please Edna very much,' she added with some satisfaction, looking at the widow.

Gathering that there wasn't much love lost in that direction, Ginny would have changed the subject, but her other aunt said, 'And your father was so looking forward to the birth of Venetia's child and being a grandfather. He invited her and Alex here several times after their wedding, just for the odd day and a couple of weekends, you know. But I think they'd started to become close again. Such a tragedy when she died. We all felt it.'

'Yes.' Ginny's face had become a beautiful, closed mask.

Her aunt had opened her mouth to ask Ginny why she hadn't been at Venetia's funeral, but slowly closed it again when she saw the withdrawal in her face. Hastily changing the subject, she said, 'Did you know that your father gave the house in Bath to Venetia as a wedding present?'

'No. No, I didn't.' Not wanting to talk about her sister any more, Ginny asked after her cousins, who weren't present, and was soon safely involved in family news.

After an hour or so, when Ginny was thinking of leaving, her mother came over to her. 'We've hardly had a chance to talk. Where are you staying?'

'Nowhere, at the moment. I hired a car at the airport and came straight here.'

'You must come home with me, then,' Mrs Barclay said firmly. 'How long can you stay in England?'

'I'm not sure, yet,' Ginny replied cautiously. She was pleased to see her mother, but knew from experience that she could only stand a few days of her continuous company before their personalities began to grate. And Mrs Barclay had a habit of arranging parties or accepting invitations for Ginny without asking her first. But she had always done it so there was no hope of changing her now.

'You might as well drive me home, then. I'll tell Alex. I expect he'll be glad to leave.'

Ginny watched her mother thread her way across the room, stopping for a word with a couple of people on the way but eventually reaching Alex's side. Not as tall as her daughter, she had to tilt her head to look at Alex, who was well over six feet. They spoke for a few minutes and then Alex looked across at Ginny. She met his glance levelly, not turning away from the scorn in his eyes. Then her mother beckoned her over.

'Ginny, I left my umbrella in Alex's car; will you go and get it for me? And you can bring your car back here at the same time, can't you?'

Having thus pushed them into a situation neither wanted, she turned away to chat happily to an old and dear friend she hadn't seen for sixteen years or so.

'Are you leaving now?' Ginny asked Alex. He nodded with cold reluctance. 'I'll get my coat, then.'

They set out from the house to walk back to the church, physically side by side, but with strong mental antagonism emanating from Alex. They walked in silence for a while, until Ginny said, 'Mother tells me you're still working with Jeff. How is he?'

'I take it that's just an idle social enquiry,' Alex answered with freezing sarcasm. 'If you'd really cared how he was you could have answered the letters Jeff sent to you after you went away.'

'I did answer a couple of them, but as I didn't expect to ever see him again there didn't seem to be much point in continuing to write. Breaks are better if they're made clean,' she retorted. And his letters had always contained news of Alex and Venetia, news she hadn't wanted to hear.

'Yes, I'm still working with him, and no, he still isn't married. Is that what you wanted to know?'

His abrupt tone made her fall silent again, afraid that anything she said would only get her head snapped off. She couldn't think of anything more to say, anyway, nothing that wouldn't bring back painful memories for one or other of them. Most of her memories about Alex were painful, she realised, with one very notable exception. But even that had been gained by deceit.

The church, with its tower crowned by a short, stubby spike, was in view before either of them spoke again, and then it was Alex who said with curt reluctance, 'Your mother said you weren't sure how long you were going to be over here.'

'No, my plans aren't settled yet,' Ginny answered in some surprise.

'There's some business I'd like to discuss with you before you go back to America.'

'What business?'

Alex frowned at her directness. 'My solicitor wrote to you after Venetia died.' He got the last two words out all right, but there was bleak unhappiness in his eyes. 'She named you in her will.'

'Yes, I remember.'

'But you didn't reply,' he pointed out brusquely.

'No.' There was no point in telling him that she had been too ill to cope with anything for several weeks and that afterwards she just couldn't bring herself to answer the letter.

His tone infinitely sarcastic, Alex said, 'I dare say now that you're so successful, and presumably affluent, anything Venetia left you would be a mere bagatelle, but the things meant a lot to Venetia and she wanted you to have them.'

Her body beginning to tremble, Ginny turned up the high collar of her coat and held it together, hiding her face. Her free hand she stuffed into her pocket, balled into a tight fist, her nails digging into the cut on her palm. 'What do you want me to do about them?' she asked shortly, determined not to let him see how he was hurting her.

He didn't see; he thought she was just heartless and uncaring. 'Collect them, presumably—if you have time before you have to rush back to your terribly important career,' Alex sneered.

A sudden rush of anger filled her, warming, life-saving. It flared in her eyes as she turned her head to look at him. 'Yes, it is important to me. Just as yours is to you, presumably. What are you doing now, Alex—still teaching at a university? Still reading papers about lasers at boring conferences? The same things after all these years?'

Her taunt got to him. His mouth thinned into a hard, set line. 'That's right. Still trying to find ways of making the world better for parasites like you.'

It was obvious that she wasn't going to win this argument. Ginny had reached her car and stopped beside it. 'Presumably Mother has your phone number. I'll give you a ring when it's convenient for me to come and pick up the things.'

'Speak to my solicitor,' Alex said curtly, and, taking a card from his wallet, he wrote down the name of the firm on the back. He handed it to her and Ginny expected him to walk to his car, but Alex hesitated, a grim look in his eyes.

'Is there something else?'

He shoved his hands in the pockets of his overcoat. She noticed that his face was thinner than she remembered. His expression was different, too; there were lines around his mouth as if it was often twisted with pain, and he had lost the look of enthusiasm and love of life that he'd used to have. She hadn't seen him smile today but Ginny was sure that when he did his eyes wouldn't crinkle as they used to. There were grey flecks in his hair, too, that hadn't been there five years ago.

'Venetia left you all her personal possessions,' he told her, hating having to say it. 'That included the house your father gave her as a wedding present.'

Ginny gave him a startled look. 'Are you sure?'

'Yes, of course I'm damn well sure!' Annoyed at his own outburst, Alex pursed his lips. 'It's right that the house should be left to you, as it was given by your father. But—I'd like to buy it from you.'

'Why?'

He gave a derisive snort. 'You always did come right out with that word. Think about it: Venetia and I lived there together. It holds a great many memories for me. Memories that I don't want you trampling all over,' he said insultingly. 'I don't want you dirtying it. I don't want to think of you bringing your playboy lovers back to a place where we were happy.'

His words hurt like knife-thrusts but Ginny was much too proud to let him see. 'I really don't think I have any playboy lovers at the moment,' she said sardonically.

But Alex could take her sarcasm and cap it. 'But then you've only been in England half a day, which hardly gives even you time to find any,' he said mockingly.

He thought he'd had the last word and turned away, but Ginny called after him, 'I thought you'd have been intelligent enough not to believe everything you read in the papers, Alex. And you really should learn not to insult someone you want to do business with.'

Honour satisfied by that riposte, Ginny turned to unlock her car, but before she could turn the key Alex strode back and caught hold of her arm, swinging her round. 'Don't think I want to,' he said savagely. 'You caused Venetia a lot of heartache by cutting yourself off from her so completely. It was the only thing that spoiled her happiness. And she had such a short time, so few years before she was killed.'

His words brought all the pain back, made her bleed inside. To hide it Ginny said the first thing that came into her head, and said it flippantly. 'Venetia always was a lousy driver.'

Pure rage transfigured Alex's face. Lifting his hand, he struck her hard across the face. Then he stood back, his body shaking, his hands clenched tightly, fighting for control. 'Dear God! The first time I've ever hit a woman and it has to be a little slut like you.' He turned then and walked away, stumbling as he did so, as if he was ill. Reaching his car, he leaned against it for a moment before pulling out the keys and opening the door. He didn't look at her again. Just got in and drove past, his knuckles white as they gripped the steering-wheel, his profile a stone-like mask.

Ginny watched him go before getting slowly into the car. The collar of her coat had taken most of the force of his blow but when she looked into the mirror she could see a pink mark on her cheek. Some careful work with the contents of her make-up bag removed it, and when she went back to her father's house she just looked a little more tanned than before. Her mother certainly didn't notice anything, but when they got in the car to drive home she looked all round the interior and said, 'Where's my umbrella?'

'Your what? Oh, that!' Ginny gave her a bemused look and then burst into almost hysterical laughter.

It was a few days before Ginny got round to phoning Alex's solicitor, but he knew all about her so Alex must have been in touch earlier. 'I've been instructed by your brother-in-law to make you an offer for the house and for the personal items left to you by his late wife,' the solicitor told her, his voice businesslike, devoid of sensitivity. He named the sum, adding that the price for the house had been arrived at by a neutral estate agent, but Ginny had been away from England so long that she'd lost touch with house prices and didn't know whether it was fair or not.

'Obviously I can't make up my mind without first seeing the house.'

'I can send you a copy of the estate agent's estimate. And if you wish to send your own valuer along to have a look at the house I can arrange for him to inspect it.'

'Thank you, but I'd like to look at the house myself.'

'You really needn't put yourself to the trouble, Miss Barclay. I can send you——'

'Look, it is my house, isn't it?' Ginny broke in, beginning to be annoyed.

'Why, yes. But Mr Warwick—well, he . . .'

His voice trailed off and Ginny guessed that Alex had told him to try to keep her away, to conduct the business by letter. 'I shall go to see the house tomorrow morning,' Ginny said firmly. 'Please arrange for someone to meet me there at eleven o'clock to let me in. What's the address?'

He gave it to her, with instructions on how to reach it, his voice still reluctant. 'Mr Warwick may ask me to send someone from this office,' he told her before he rang off.

The cold winds that had blown on the day of her father's funeral had died away and the drive to Bath from her mother's home near Cheltenham was a pleasant one through sunlit countryside. Ginny drove carefully, concentrating on driving on the left-hand side of the road instead of the right. Most of the time it was OK, but sometimes, when she came to dual carriageways and roundabouts, she had to reverse actions that had become automatic. Bath was a beautiful town; she knew it well and had always loved it. As children she and Venetia had been taken there often to see the museums, the ancient Roman Baths, and the beautiful Georgian stone buildings built to provide suitable houses for the nobles and gentry who had come there to take the waters.

She arrived early and spent a little time driving round the town just for the pleasure of seeing again

the perfect architectural lines of Queen's Square, the
Circus and the Royal Crescent. But at ten to eleven
Ginny consulted the instructions the solicitor had
given her and drove away from the grander part of
town to a street which consisted of a long terrace of
smaller Georgian houses, their front doors giving directly on to the pavement. Pulling up outside number
sixty-two, Ginny turned off the engine and looked at
the house. There were a couple of worn stone steps
going up to a white-painted front door with a fanlight
above it, and to the right of the door there was a sash
window, still the original by the look of it. The house
came as no surprise. It was the kind of house that
Venetia would have loved, and Ginny could imagine
her sister painting walls and hanging curtains,
choosing furniture and carpets, eager to make the
house into a home for her and Alex. They were mental
pictures that she had seen often before, her close em-
pathy with her twin having brought them vividly into
her mind many times when Venetia was alive.

Getting slowly out of the car, Ginny stood on the
pavement, trying again to recapture her sister's spirit.
She felt closer to her here, far more than at her grave,
but she wasn't sure whether Venetia wanted her here
or not.

There was no one waiting outside to meet her.
Straightening her shoulders a little, Ginny walked
across the pavement, up the steps and rang the bell.
There was dust on the framework of the door panels,
she noticed, and the windows wanted cleaning. Evidently Alex wasn't very house-proud—or perhaps he
just didn't care any more.

She had expected a stranger, someone sent by the
solicitor, to open the door, but it was Alex. Ginny's

eyes widened in surprise and, disconcerted, she began to turn away.

'It's all right,' Alex said abruptly. 'You don't have to be afraid.' He held the door wide and stepped back. 'You'd better come in.'

Slowly Ginny did so, her eyes on his face. There was a haggard look about his features, as if he hadn't been sleeping. They both spoke at once.

'Look, you don't have to show me round yourself——'

'I must apologise for hitting you——'

Alex had spoken woodenly, and Ginny gave him a questioning glance, wondering why he was putting himself through this. 'It's all right,' she said with a shrug. 'You didn't hurt me.'

His mouth twisted wryly. 'No, I don't suppose I did.' And, before she could guess at his meaning, he went on, 'I apologise, all the same. It was— unnecessary.'

A strange word to describe an instant of black fury. 'I apologise, too,' Ginny said. 'I didn't mean to upset you. Look, I can go round the house by myself; there's no need for you to——'

'No.' He gave a decisive shake of his head. 'I want to be here. I don't want you—I don't want to think of you going through her things.'

They were still standing in the hallway, but now Ginny took a couple of steps into the house before turning to face him again. 'She was my sister, Alex. I loved her, too.'

'Really?' There was deep scorn in his voice.

'Yes, I did. And she loved me. Would she have left me this house and her things otherwise?'

'She left them to you because she felt guilty about you. About your going away and cutting yourself off.'

Ginny frowned, then shook her head. 'No, I don't buy that. There was no guilt between us.'

'How would you know how Venetia felt?' Alex said on a sneer. 'You didn't even bother to write to her.'

It was no good trying to explain the closeness of the bond that had been between them, the almost telepathic awareness of emotions; anyone who hadn't experienced a similar bond would never understand. And maybe he was right, after all. Maybe Venetia had experienced some guilt feelings; the mental telepathy between the twins hadn't been so strong during the last year of Venetia's life—not until the very end. 'Are you going to show me the house?' Ginny asked shortly.

Alex's face tightened, but he gave a brief nod and led her into a room on the right of the hall. 'This is the sitting-room.'

It was a pretty room with light wallpaper and matching curtains, a comfortable sofa by the window and an armchair either side of the fire. There were pictures on the walls and ornaments on shelves. But Ginny felt as if everything she saw was out of focus because of the thick layer of dust that lay everywhere. No, not quite everywhere; there was a clear trail across the carpet where someone had walked often and a clean patch on the chair on the left side of the fireplace where someone had sat. Instinctively she knew that this was where Alex came to mourn his lost wife and child.

'You don't live here,' Ginny said tightly, searching for normality.

'No, I have rooms at the university.' He opened a double door on the far side of the room. 'This leads through to the dining-room. When the house was built it used to have a marvellous view over open fields to the hills, but now——' he gestured and shrugged '—as you see.'

Walking to the window, Ginny looked down on to an overgrown, narrow garden about ten feet below, bordered by high walls, and beyond the far wall there were the unlovely modern roofs of a retail and trading estate.

'The kitchen is downstairs.'

Going back to the hall, Alex went ahead of her down a rather steep staircase to the lower floor. The house, she realised, must be built on the side of a hill, as there was no sign of this lower floor from the front. The kitchen must have been warm and attractive when the house was lived in. The fittings were of natural wood and there were lots of copper and brass utensils hung on the walls, but they had lost their lustre now.

'There's a scullery that we turned into a laundry-room, and a room that used to be a servant's room that we just used to store junk.' Alex's voice was quite unemotional as he pushed open doors and held them so that she could look in.

'Yes. I see.'

Turning, he went back up the stairs and then climbed the much wider flight to the rooms on the top floor. 'There's just the bathroom and two bedrooms on this floor,' he said brusquely.

'What's up those stairs?' Ginny pointed to a narrow, boxed-in staircase that led up between two rooms. Not because she much wanted to know, but because she could feel Alex's growing tension.

'The attic. It used to be used as a servant's bedroom, but now it just has the water tanks.' Ginny nodded and waited for him to open the door to one of the bedrooms, but his jaw thrust forward and Alex burst out, 'I offered you a more than fair price for the house. Why couldn't you just accept it? You don't have any real interest in it—you've just come here to satisfy your curiosity.'

'Perhaps,' Ginny surprised him by agreeing. 'I wanted to see the place where Venetia lived. I wanted to see if I'd got them right.'

'Got what right?' Alex asked with a frown.

'The pictures I had of the place.'

'But you never wrote to each other; Venetia couldn't have sent you any photographs of the house. Unless your mother——'

Ginny shook her head decisively. 'Not photographs, I meant mental pictures.' She saw the derision in Alex's eyes and said mildly, 'You can hardly expect me not to have formed some sort of mental picture of Venetia's house. We were always very close, you know.' She could see by the curl of his lip that Alex found the idea distasteful, so she said, 'I take it that door leads to the main bedroom?'

'As it's the door to the front bedroom that's hardly difficult to guess,' Alex answered shortly. 'I suppose you want to go in there.'

'If you'd rather I came back alone some other time...'

'No,' he answered brusquely. 'Let's get this over with.' He pushed open the door and walked in, leaving her to follow.

The room had pale blue walls and a white carpet. The bed was big and old-fashioned; Victorian, Ginny guessed. Made of polished wood, it was covered by a patchwork quilt in shades of blue that Venetia must have made. Ginny quickly turned her eyes away from the bed, guessing that Alex hated her seeing the place where he and Venetia had made love. And it must have reminded him, too, of the time when he had taken Ginny to his bed. Just once. Such a long time ago. Ginny's eyes went to the floor. In this room, too, there was a trail of footprints in the dust. They led to the bed, and there was an indentation where someone had lain.

'Why don't you look after the place?' Ginny said, suddenly fierce. 'Venetia would hate it to be like this.'

'Mind your own damn business.'

But she hardly heard him. Walking over to the built-in wardrobe, Ginny pulled open the door to reveal all Venetia's clothes and shoes still in their place. And her make-up bag and bottles of perfumes and lotions were still on the dressing-table in front of the window. Her portrait, a blown-up studio photograph that had been part of their portfolio when Venetia, too, had been a model before her marriage, hung over the fireplace. But Ginny hardly glanced at it; she saw the identical face in the mirror every day.

'You've turned this house into a mausoleum,' she said angrily. 'A shrine.'

'No.' Alex bit the word out, but then put his hands up to his face, and wiped them over it as if wiping away emotion, feelings. Lifting his head, his jaw thrust forward, he said, 'After Venetia died I had no use for the place. She'd left it to you, together with all her things, but you didn't bother to reply to my letter, so I couldn't clear it. I just took my own things out and shut the door on it.'

'But you come back.'

Alex nodded, the lines about his mouth deepening. 'I come here to remember. We were so very happy here.' He turned abruptly away. 'The bathroom is at the back.'

The bathroom had a big, old-fashioned iron bath that stood on clawed feet and jutted out from the wall. It looked like fun, but apart from that the room was pretty utilitarian. On the landing, Alex hesitated, but then went to open the door to the other bedroom.

'That's the nursery,' Ginny said. 'She never finished it.'

He gave her a strange look, almost one of dread. 'No.' Slowly he turned the knob and pushed open the door.

Ginny went to step inside but stopped on the threshold and then turned quickly away. There was no need to go in; Ginny had found what she was looking for. Her sister's spirit was here in this unfinished room where her child would have lain.

'Don't you want to see it?' Alex jeered as she pushed past him. 'Don't tell me you're actually feeling something at last.'

Ginny rounded on him in a cold fury of anger. 'Strange as it may seem, you don't have the monopoly of grief, Alex. When Venetia died, half of me died, too.'

He laughed at that, a loud, derisive laugh of bitter disbelief. 'Oh, yes,' he said in mocking scorn. 'You felt her loss so much that you couldn't even come to her funeral.'

'Yes,' Ginny bit back. 'That's exactly why I couldn't come. I felt her loss. I felt her hurt. I felt her pain. Everything that Venetia felt when she crashed, I felt.

I know that she tried to fight, tried desperately for your sake, but the injuries were too great.' Ginny's voice had sunk almost to a whisper, the bleak remembrance of black despair in her eyes. 'And when she died, when I felt the life go out of her, then I wanted to die, too. There was nothing to live for and we had been so close all our lives, so very close. Sharing everything. I didn't want to go on living without her.'

Alex frowned, his eyes fixed on her face. 'What are you saying?'

She glanced at him and gave a mirthless laugh. 'I didn't go to Venetia's funeral because I—I had a nervous breakdown. The doctors gave it some fancy name but what it boiled down to was that I had suffered everything that Venetia had gone through, and I——' her voice faltered '—I nearly died, too.'

CHAPTER TWO

'You had a nervous breakdown!'

'Yes.' Ginny nodded, putting a hand up to her face. 'I was in a clinic for several weeks before I recovered—physically recovered.'

Alex shook his head incredulously. 'I can't believe it.'

'Don't, then,' Ginny snapped back, and she turned to run down the stairs.

But Alex caught her up in the hall and grabbed her arm, swinging her round. 'If you'd had a nervous breakdown your mother would have known about it.'

'She was already terribly upset over Venetia's death. I wasn't about to add to that by letting her know that I was ill. So I told my—my agent to tell anyone who asked that I was away, working on an assignment.' A shudder of remembrance ran through her and Ginny closed her eyes tightly for a moment. When she opened them she slowly lifted her head and looked at Alex, then stiffened. 'You don't believe me, do you? Damn it, Alex, do you really think that anything else would have kept me away from Venetia's funeral?'

He gave her a narrow, withdrawn look. 'What I don't believe is that you could feel the physical pain that Venetia experienced. Why, she was a couple of thousand miles away. How could you possibly——?'

'I don't know how,' Ginny cut in angrily. 'I only know that I did.'

'But it's impossible.'

Ginny flashed him a scathing look. 'Yes, of course. As you say; it's impossible.'

Alex's face hardened. 'You always did have a vivid imagination. Or maybe you liked the idea—or your agent did. In the world you move in it would probably have made a good story.'

Ginny flushed. 'I only told you because you're so obviously obsessed by the fact that I didn't go to the funeral. Well, now you know why.'

'Any publicity is good publicity, is that it?' Alex's voice was scathing again.

'No one else knows,' Ginny said in throbbing anger, her fists clenched. 'No one but you. And now I don't much care that you don't believe me.' Reaching for the front door, she yanked it open and ran down the steps.

'What about the house?' Alex strode up to her as Ginny fumbled for her car keys.

She gave him a fulminating glance, then turned to look back at the house. 'It's mine, isn't it? And everything in it?'

'Except for some of the furniture, yes.'

'Then please arrange to have everything that still belongs to you removed by the end of the week. I am *not* going to sell you the house, and I want you out. And you can tell your solicitor to send me a set of keys at once.'

Alex's face whitened. 'Ginny, you can't...'

'Oh, but I can. Haven't you just more or less told me that I'm capable of anything? Well, if I can fake a nervous breakdown, then I can damn well do this!'

And she got in the car and drove away, leaving him standing on the pavement looking after her.

Alex wanted the house too badly to leave it there. Ginny had hardly got back to her mother's before the solicitor called again and said that Alex was willing to increase his offer for the house. 'Tell him I'm not interested,' Ginny answered, biting back a stronger reply. 'I shall come to your office at ten o'clock next Monday to pick up the keys.' And she put the phone down on his continuing persuasions.

The solicitor rang twice more, but Ginny just said, 'Tell him no,' without bothering to listen. But on Thursday evening Alex sent Jeff Ferguson over to see her.

She had first met Jeff over five years ago, on a blind date. A university lecturer in history, he had worked at the same red-brick university as Alex, who had shared a bachelor pad with him and brought him along one night to make up a foursome with herself and Venetia. He was nice, fun, and Ginny liked him, and Jeff had been keen on Ginny. If he could, he would have been a lot more than keen, but he had quickly realised that both the twins were equally crazy about Alex. His friendship had helped her at that terribly difficult time, and Ginny still had a soft spot for him. She was sitting on the wide window-seat in her mother's sitting-room when he arrived, a note-pad resting against her knees, a pen in her hand, but her thoughts roaming from the letter she was trying to write.

The sound of a car drawing up outside attracted her fickle attention and she watched as Jeff got out.

It was only about six o'clock and the sun was still out though low in the sky, with that fierce brightness of a spring evening. After getting out of the car, Jeff stood looking at the house for a moment. He was still as thin as ever, but he didn't look so much like a gangling schoolboy now. Perhaps it was because his suit fitted him better; maybe he'd found a good tailor. As she watched he raised a hand to brush a fall of thick fair hair off his forehead and to push his glasses back up his nose. It was the latter nervous gesture that brought a smile of remembrance to Ginny's lips and made her drop the note-pad and hurry to the door to meet him.

'Jeff. Hi. How are you?' She gave him a big grin and held out her hands to him.

He returned the grin, taking her hands and holding them tightly for a moment. 'I'm fine. And you're looking even more beautiful than I remember.'

'Watch it—flattery will get you anywhere. Come on in.' Ginny led him back into the sitting-room. 'This calls for a drink. What will you have?'

'Well, perhaps a G and T, please.'

'Great, I'll join you.' Ginny poured out the gin and tonics and turned to hand him one. His eyes were going over her slim figure in the long trousers and fluffy white sweater. A faint flush of colour came into his cheeks when he realised she'd caught him looking. 'I hear you're at Bristol with Alex now,' Ginny said to put him at ease.

'Yes, I followed him there a year or so after he and Venetia got married.'

'And do you like it?' Ginny sat down on the window-seat again and gestured to him to join her. 'You must tell me all about it.'

But he remained standing. 'I'd like to. And preferably over dinner somewhere. But I've got to tell you first that—well, I didn't just come here to see you. Although I wanted to, of course. But I've been sent.'

Ginny took a swallow of her drink. 'By Alex, presumably.'

'Yes.' Jeff hesitated, then shrugged. 'You can guess why; he wants me to mediate for him, try and persuade you to let him buy the house from you.'

'And do you think you'll succeed?'

Jeff laughed. 'Not for a minute. I'm his last-ditch attempt.'

'But you agreed to come and try, all the same.'

He nodded, his eyes on her face. 'As I said, I wanted to see you again.'

'But you wanted to help Alex more,' Ginny said shrewdly.

He pushed his glasses up his nose, then came to sit beside her. 'You didn't see Alex after Venetia died.' Ginny gave him a sharp look, but there was no condemnation in his face or tone, only a kind of pity. 'He was in shock at first and bottled everything up inside. In his work at the university, in his dealings with people, you'd never have guessed what had happened if you didn't know. But as the weeks and months went by you could see the change in him. Grief was gnawing away at him from the inside. He had shut the house up and moved out of it immediately, but I managed to get him to go back there on some pretext and I think it was only then, in those surroundings, that he was able to finally give way to his feelings.'

'You've been a good friend to him,' Ginny said warmly.

Jeff looked surprised. 'I did what I could for him. He would have done the same for me.'

'But you haven't married, and you're not engaged or anything?'

'No.' He gave her a slow grin. 'Stop trying to divert me from the subject.' He became serious again. 'Alex obviously feels that he still needs that house, that he needs a place where he can go and grieve in peace and solitude.'

Ginny gave him a contemplative look, thinking over what he'd said, but then shook her head decisively. 'It's been over two years, Jeff. Have you been to that house? He's turning it into some kind of shrine, and that isn't healthy. If he wants to grieve he can do it in his heart; he doesn't need a special place.'

'I'm not so sure.'

'But I am. When you lose someone you love dearly the loss is always with you, you can't shake it off, and for a long while it hits you at the strangest times, but then you learn how to control it so that you can take it out and mourn when you're alone for a little while. But you don't need a special place to do that. It can be lying in bed at night, or on a plane, or walking through a park. Anywhere.'

'You speak as if you know.'

'Of course I know,' Ginny answered with sudden anger. 'Venetia was my twin sister; there will never be anyone as close to me as she was.'

'Sorry.' He pushed at his glasses. 'It's strange seeing you; you and Venetia are—were—so alike. It's almost like her coming back to life.'

'I suppose you saw quite a lot of her after she was married?'

'Yes, she was always inviting me round for dinner and often she'd invite another girl along.' He grinned. 'She was always trying to marry me off. Felt sorry for me, I suppose.'

'Perhaps she just wanted you to be as happy as she and Alex were,' Ginny said gently.

'Yes.' Jeff turned round a little on the seat so that he could look at her directly. 'And what about you? Are you happy in your career? Have you—got over Alex?'

That was a question she'd expected and Ginny laughed easily. 'After all this time? Of course. You meet some very dishy men in my profession, you know.'

'Yes, you've become quite famous.'

'I suppose you mean infamous. You've been reading the gossip columns, Jeff.'

'Well, your name has been linked with some well-known men.'

'Of course. It's all good publicity.' She spoke lightly, humorously, but there was no laughter in her eyes.

'You must find England very boring after New York.'

She looked at him and realised they were back to a personal level. Reaching out, Ginny put her hand on his arm. 'Why don't you take me out to dinner and you can tell me all that you've been doing while I've been away? Have you been duping any more tourists the way you did at that exhibition we went to? I've always remembered that.'

Jeff grinned. 'Yes, that was a good day.'

Soon they were in a reminiscent mood as they ate Indian food at a restaurant in Cheltenham. But they hadn't known each other all that long and had only been out together for a few times, so they didn't have that many memories to recall. And Jeff's life at the university didn't take that long to cover, especially as he was rather modest about his scholastic achievements.

'I'm booked to go on a dig in Italy this summer,' he told her. 'I'm trying to persuade Alex to come along, but it isn't really his thing.'

No, Ginny couldn't imagine Alex spending endless hours on his knees scraping away at an excavation. Not for a holiday, anyway; he was far too full of vigorous energy. 'What does he usually do?' she asked.

'Well, he and Venetia used to go skiing in the winter and to places where they could go in for water sports like wind-surfing in the summer. They took me along a couple of times, but I usually managed to find a few ruins to go off and have a look at.'

'You were obviously very close to them. I'm glad.'

'Mmm.' A sad look came into Jeff's eyes. 'I haven't any family of my own, but they made me feel as if I was a part of theirs. I never felt that I was intruding.' He gave her a direct look. 'But Venetia missed you. She tried to hide it from Alex, but I know she did. She often used to talk to me about you, especially if there had been something about you in the papers or a picture of you in a magazine. She was very proud of your success, you know.'

Ginny looked away. 'That's nice.'

Jeff hesitated, looking at her averted profile, then said, 'Venetia told me why you went away. That Alex found out it was you he'd—he'd spent the night with and not Venetia. She told me everything: how it was you who'd originally met Alex on the plane, but she'd taken your place when he came to London looking for you. I knew that you were both in love with him, of course, but until she told me I hadn't realised that you had the—prior claim, so to speak.'

'Did she tell you how we decided which one of us would stay and which leave?'

He nodded. 'Yes, she told me you tossed a coin to decide.'

Ginny gave him a thoughtful look out of her long-lashed hazel eyes. 'Does Alex know that?'

'I'm not sure. He's never mentioned it to me, but then he probably wouldn't.'

'I don't think that he can know. I can't see Venetia telling him something like that; however much he loved her, he wouldn't like it,' she said contemplatively.

Looking at her face as she spoke of Alex, Jeff could see no emotion in her eyes; her features wore the cool detachment of the top model that she was. Curious, he said, 'If you have no feelings about Alex now, why won't you let him buy the house from you?'

She glanced at him for a moment. 'Has it occurred to either of you, I wonder, that Venetia might have left me that house for a purpose? Oh, I know Alex thinks it was because she felt guilty about my being the one to go away, but there might have been another reason, you know.'

'What reason?'

Deciding that she didn't want to confide completely in Jeff, Ginny shrugged and said, 'Because it was given to her by our father and she wanted it to stay in our family, of course.'

'I see. Not because she thought you might come back here and get together with Alex again?' he said perceptively.

Her chin came up at that and Ginny said in a cold, keep-off voice, 'Somehow I can't imagine Venetia thinking on those lines.'

'Why not? That was the real reason you had in mind, wasn't it?'

For a moment Ginny couldn't decide whether to be angry or not, then she gave a small sigh and grinned. 'You always were good at reading my mind.'

'It's not as easy as it used to be. Five years ago you were an open book; now——' he pushed his glasses on his nose again as he contemplated her '—now you've built a wall around yourself. You're cool and self-possessed. A career woman. But underneath I think you're even more vulnerable than you were.'

'A psychologist, no less,' Ginny said on a sarcastic note, not best pleased at being analysed—and analysed so accurately.

'And *is* that why you're going to keep the house? So that you and Alex can——'

'No,' Ginny broke in sharply. 'If you must know, I'm keeping the house because Alex made me damn angry. If he hadn't been so rude to me I might have let him have it without even seeing the place. But now that I have seen it I'm going to keep it. I don't like the way he's neglected it.'

'And am I to tell him that?'

Annoyed, Ginny said, 'Ah, yes, I forgot you were just the messenger-boy. Sure, tell him by all means. And tell him to stop wasting his time and mine by trying to get me to change my mind.'

'But he goes there when things get him down. It's a kind of—of sanctuary for him.'

'Then it's about time he snapped out of it,' Ginny said firmly. 'And you can tell him that, too, for all I care.' She pushed her chair back and stood up. 'Let's go, shall we?'

On Monday morning Ginny loaded up her car with her luggage, said goodbye to her mother, and drove into Bath. She hadn't heard anything else from Alex and hoped that he'd given up at last, but when she arrived at the solicitor's office to pick up the keys Alex was sitting in the waiting-room. He tossed aside the paper he'd been reading and stood up as she came in.

Ginny came to an abrupt halt in the doorway. 'For heaven's sake, I've already told you——'

'It's all right, you needn't start getting annoyed,' Alex said shortly. 'As Venetia's executor I have to be here to sign the house over to you.'

Her shoulders relaxing, Ginny said, 'I see.'

She went to a chair on the opposite side of the room from Alex and sat down, crossing her long, shapely legs at the ankle. Her hair was drawn back into a roll at her neck and she was wearing a deep red tailored suit with a short skirt. She looked cool and sophisticated, and very beautiful. Alex didn't sit down again; he looked her over, then went to the window and stood with his back to her, looking out.

'Something rivetingly interesting out there, is there?' Ginny said into the silence.

A glint of humour came into his eyes as he turned to face her, but was instantly gone. 'Jeff passed on your message. It seems that I have only myself to blame for your insisting on keeping the house. You're doing it out of perverseness.' Ginny didn't bother to answer that, and Alex's jaw thrust forward as he burst out, 'You can have no possible use for it. You'll be going back to America before long, and then what will become of the place? Will you let it? Or sell it? The house where we lived, were happy? Are you going to let strangers sleep in our bed, touch Venetia's things?'

'I haven't yet made up my mind what I'm going to do with the house,' Ginny said calmly. 'When I do, I'll let you know. And if I do eventually decide to sell it I will of course give you the first refusal.'

He looked surprised, as if he hadn't even expected that much from her. 'And in the meantime?'

Ginny was saved from answering as a girl came in and told them that the solicitor was ready to see them.

The formalities didn't take long, and afterwards Alex took a set of keys from his pocket and was about to hand them to her but then changed his mind and put them on the desk in front of them. Ginny looked at the keys and slowly reached out to pick them up. She felt, strangely, as if this action was one of the most momentous in her life, that by stretching out her hand and picking up the keys she was deliberately altering the course of it. Just as the toss of a coin had altered it five years ago. Gripping the keys hard, so that they bit into her palm, Ginny cursed herself for a fool and said briskly, 'Is that everything? Thank you.' She stood up and shook hands with the solicitor, turned and walked out of the office.

Alex caught her up on the pavement outside. 'Are you going back to the house now?'

'Yes.'

'I'd like to come back with you. There are several things you ought to know about the house.'

'All right.' Ginny's voice was again cool and brisk. 'My car's in the car park down the road.'

They walked together to it, side by side, but carefully not touching, and Ginny tried to recall how many times they had ever walked together like this. There was the first time of course, when she had met Alex on the plane to Paris, she on her way to do a modelling shoot, he going to catch a connecting flight to take him to Stockholm where he was to read a paper at a conference. They had walked together then from the plane through the terminal building to where their ways had parted to go through different Customs points. They had arranged to meet afterwards but Alex hadn't been allowed into the main concourse of the airport to join her because he was a transit passenger. Ginny had waited and then given him up, just missing the messenger he sent to find her. But Alex hadn't given up; even though he hadn't known her name, he had written to every model agency in London to try and trace her. But Ginny had been still away and Venetia had got the letter and gone to meet him instead, not telling him she wasn't the girl that he'd met originally.

That had been the first time, Ginny remembered. They had gone jogging together once after that, but

the next real time when they had walked together had
been when Ginny had duped Alex into thinking she
was Venetia and she had gone out for the evening with
him. She had intended to tell him, later, who she really
was, but the wonderful evening had lengthened into
an incredibly magical night of the most sensuous,
passionate lovemaking, and Ginny had known that
she could never spoil it by telling him the truth.

But he had found out, of course, and had been
lividly angry with both sisters, telling them he never
wanted to see either of them again. And it was then
that she and Venetia had agreed that their only chance
of one of them getting him back was if the other went
right away and never came back. And they had tossed
a coin to see which one of them should go. Even now,
the memory of that traumatic time sent a quiver of
emotion running through her, but none of her feelings
showed in Ginny's face. Anyone watching them, and
there were many who looked, saw only a tall and outwardly serene young woman, who walked with the
long-legged grace of a model, and beside her an even
taller man, darkly handsome, but with a grim, withdrawn look about his mouth.

When they reached the car Ginny unlocked it and
drove the short distance to the house in silence. Some
of the furniture had gone: the sofa in the sitting-room
and the dining-room table and chairs, but there was
still quite a lot left, even the bed in the main bedroom.
Ginny looked round and Alex followed her, but they
didn't speak until she turned to him with questioning
eyes. 'Didn't you want the bed?'

'It isn't mine. Venetia found it in an auction sale
and restored it herself. She enjoyed doing that, and

bought all the other bits of furniture that are still here in the same way.'

Ginny nodded. 'She used to do that when we lived in London. There were several pieces of furniture in the flat that she'd restored.'

'They're all here, along with the others.'

Turning to look at him, Ginny said, 'But the money she used to buy them with must have been yours.'

Alex shook his head. 'She used the money she earned from a modelling class she ran.'

Ginny hadn't known that Venetia had taught modelling. It added another aspect to her life. And she could imagine her twin happily carrying back home her finds at the auction sales, to make them beautiful and enhance her home. 'I'll arrange for the bed to be sent to you,' And, before he could say anything, 'You've taken everything else that's yours?'

'Yes. But there are some other things that belong to you. I didn't leave them here in case the place was burgled, or squatters moved in.' He had a briefcase with him—he opened it and took out several small boxes. 'This is all Venetia's jewellery. They count as her personal possessions, and so come to you.'

He began to open the boxes and place them on a small table. Ginny stared. Some of the things she recognised, of course. They were presents that had been given to her twin for birthdays and Christmas, and often Ginny had been given the identical piece. But there was a locket, a beautiful pearl choker, and some gold chains and bracelets; Venetia must have been given them since her marriage. And Alex was the one who must have given them to her. One of the bracelets was made up of gold links with a few small charms hanging from it, and Ginny guessed that Alex must have bought Venetia a charm for every holiday or wedding anniversary; that was why there were so few, so very few. Last of all he opened a ring box and Ginny saw Venetia's engagement ring.

'I kept her wedding-ring,' he said shortly, his voice unnaturally tense. 'But I can give you the price it cost and——'

'Don't be so damn insulting,' Ginny said shortly. 'I had no idea that these things were—were included in the legacy. Take them back, Alex. All of them.'

'She left them to you.'

'Then she made a mistake. I'm quite sure that Venetia would have wanted you to have them.'

A stubborn look came into his eyes and for a moment she was afraid that he was going to argue, but then he looked at the ring again and his face changed. 'Do you mean it?' he demanded roughly.

'*Yes*. Of course.' She looked at his face and was unable to bear the desolation in his eyes as he reached out to pick up the ring. Turning, she ran downstairs to wait for him there.

He rejoined her a few minutes later. Ginny was standing at the window in the dining-room, looking out over the garden. 'Thank you,' he said formally. 'I'm very grateful.'

Ginny turned to look at him, her hands thrust into the pockets of her jacket. 'No, you're not,' she said shrewdly. 'Right now you hate me for being here, for keeping this house from you. You hate me for looking exactly like Venetia and reminding you of her every time you see me. And most of all you hate me for being alive when she's dead.'

His eyes widened at her forthrightness but Alex didn't deny her diagnosis. 'Jeff told me all that you'd said. Including that you thought it was about time I snapped out of it.' There was harsh resentment in his tone.

'If you hadn't wanted to hear any home truths then you shouldn't have sent him,' Ginny shot back.

Alex looked as if he was going to make an equally sharp retort, but visibly restrained himself. 'I'm sorry, I didn't intend to start arguing with you again. Especially as you've given me back these.' And he gestured to the briefcase in his hand. 'I really am grateful. I owe you——'

'You owe me nothing,' Ginny cut in. 'You were going to tell me some things about the house, weren't you?'

'Yes.' Alex looked relieved by the change of subject and became businesslike. 'You'll need to know where to turn the water and electricity on. And how to light the central-heating boiler. I'll show you.'

He led the way down to the basement and for a little while they had a period that was so absolutely normal that it was like a surprise present. Alex showed her where to find the stopcocks and turned the water back on, then took off his jacket to go up into the attic to make sure that the water tanks were filling OK. 'I think you might need a new hot-water tank put in,' he called out to her as Ginny stood in the doorway. 'I was going to have it done but I—didn't get round to it. That's why I turned off the water and drained out the system; I was afraid of the place being flooded. Get ready to run downstairs and turn the stopcock off if I yell.'

'Can I help?'

'Keep your eye on the other tank as it fills.'

There was a terrific knocking and rattling of pipes as water began to run through them again. Crouching down, Ginny brushed dusty cobwebs aside as she peered at the tank. 'It looks OK.'

'Make sure there aren't any drips underneath,' Alex instructed.

Saying goodbye to her tights, Ginny knelt on the floor and peered under the tank. 'Can't see any.'

'Good; you may be OK, then.'

They both straightened up together, but Alex's warning, 'Look out,' came too late, and Ginny cracked her head on a roof beam.

'Ouch!' She staggered a little and put her hand to her head.

Alex came quickly to her side and caught her arm. 'Are you all right?'

'I—I think so. Oh, what a stupid thing to do.'

'You'd better come downstairs. Here, let me go first in case you feel faint.'

He went in front of her down the stairs, Ginny supporting herself against the wall; there wasn't any handrail. The stairs were steep and her heels high. A wave of dizziness came over her and she stood still. 'Alex.' There was alarm in her voice.

'It's OK, I've got you.' Putting his hands round her waist, Alex lifted her bodily down the rest of the flight. There was a *chaise-longue* on the landing under the window, and he sat her on it. 'Let's have a look at your head.' Parting her hair to look, he said, 'You've given it quite a bang. It's bleeding a little. Stay here and I'll get some stuff to bathe it.'

He came back with some cotton wool and a bottle of antiseptic. Ginny drew back. 'That stuff will sting.'

He grinned. 'Don't be a coward. It's for your own good, Vene——' Alex broke off abruptly, his face whitening. For a moment he stared into Ginny's eyes, each of them aghast at his mistake, but then Alex stiffened and he looked down, his hands fiercely gripping the things he was holding. A pulse beat in his jaw as he strove to control himself.

Ginny's heart was wrung with pity and she longed to reach out and touch him, to offer what comfort she could, but was sensitive enough to know that this was the last thing he wanted, so she somehow managed to say lightly, 'I wondered how long it would be before you called me that; I'm only surprised you haven't done so before.' He shot her a piercing look at that, and she said more sharply, 'Are you going to bathe my head, Alex? It's really starting to hurt now.'

'What?' Somehow he pulled himself together. 'Yes, of course. You'd—maybe it would be easier if you let your hair down.'

Ginny took out the clips, wincing a little as she touched the bump on her head. Her rich brown hair cascaded down, so long that it reached halfway down her back, and with the fine flowing waves that evoked a Pre-Raphaelite painting. Alex looked at her, his face taut with emotion, then busied himself with his task.

His hands in her hair brought back many of the sweetest memories, all of that one night they had spent together. She recalled how Alex had run his hands through her hair, then had carried it to his mouth to kiss and told her how exquisitely lovely he found it. Perhaps Alex remembered, too, for she could feel his hands trembling. But then all memories were drowned in the sharp pain of the antiseptic as he bathed her head.

Ginny gave an indignant yell. 'Hey, go easy with that stuff.'

'Sorry.' But he didn't sound it. 'Got to get any dirt out.' When he'd finished he stood back and said, 'That should be OK now. I don't think you need a plaster on it. You'd better not use a shampoo until it's healed, though.'

'Thanks,' Ginny said shortly. Taking a handkerchief from her pocket, she dabbed at the tears the pain had brought to her eyes. 'I've an idea you enjoyed doing that.'

'I didn't intend to hurt you.'

'Didn't you?' She was openly disbelieving. 'I can't help looking like Venetia, Alex.'

'But you could help coming back here,' he said sharply. Then he made an angry gesture. 'I'm sorry; you have every right to do as you please. It's just seeing you—sometimes I forget and it's almost like her being . . . being alive again.'

He took the first-aid stuff back to the bathroom and she could hear him washing his hands. When he came back, he said, 'How do you feel now?'

'My head aches, but apart from that I'm fine, thank you.' She looked at him expectantly, thinking that he would be glad to go, but Alex hesitated, something else obviously on his mind. 'Is there something else you want to tell me about the house?'

'No.' He took a couple of restless paces, but the landing was too narrow for that and he looked like a caged animal. 'I just wanted to get something straight between us,' he jerked out. 'That last time we saw each other before you went to America, when I found out the truth about our—rather triangular relationship. You said then that you were in love with me.'

Guessing what was coming, Ginny lowered her head for a moment, trying to still the beating of her heart. But then she lifted her chin, her voice and eyes cool. 'So?'

'So what I basically want to know is how you feel now.'

She stared at him, and managed an incredulous laugh. 'You want to know if I'm still in love with you?'

'Basically, yes.'

Hardly able to breathe for a great tightness in her chest, Ginny took refuge in attack. 'Why?'

Alex gave a mirthless laugh and went to sit on the stairs opposite her. He was still without his jacket, his shirt sleeves rolled up and a smudge of dirt from the attic on his shoulder. His body was as lean and athletic as ever; if anything he was thinner than when she'd first known him. Most men were supposed to put on weight after they married, but if Alex had he had certainly lost it since his widowerhood. 'It occurred to me that might have been why you'd come back,' Alex said bluntly. 'And why you want to keep the house.' His jaw thrust forward but his eyes were very cold, withdrawn. 'I thought perhaps you wanted to—go on from where we left off.'

'And if I do?' Ginny kept her eyes on his face, tilting her head a little to one side, but her fingers gripping the edge of the *chaise-longue* where the fabric had faded and frayed in the light from the window.

'Then I must tell you straight away that it's not on,' Alex returned forcefully. 'Just because I was attracted to you once, it doesn't mean that I am now. And your being Venetia's sister and looking exactly like her isn't going to make any difference. In fact, it has the opposite effect.' He paused to give weight to his words. 'Seeing you does nothing but remind me of Venetia, of my wife. And when I think of her then there's no way I want someone else.'

It suddenly struck Ginny how incongruous it was to be sitting here on this dusty little landing having this conversation, Alex in his smeared shirt and her with a bump on her head. The thought helped and she was able to let go her grip and lean back against the *chaise*, a casual arm draped across its back. And it wasn't so difficult to give a cool laugh. 'Well, I'm glad about that. Something Jeff said made me afraid you might think I still had that adolescent crush on you. Good heavens, Alex, that was years ago! I've changed completely since then. I admit I was pretty dotty over you at the time, and I'm sorry to dent your ego, but leaving England was the best move I've ever made. My career really took off in America. Living in the Big Apple is a world away from here, you know. It's an electric place, especially if you're successful.' Alex was watching her closely, studying her face, which made her give another amused laugh. 'Did you really think that was why I came home?'

'You tell me.'

'Sorry to disappoint you, Alex, darling, but quite a lot of water has gone under the bridge in my private life since then, too.'

'Or quite a lot of lovers have been in your bed since then,' Alex said in crude cruelty.

Ginny's eyes flickered, but she gave a careless shrug. 'So what's it to you?'

Alex put a hand up to his face and drew it across his chin. 'Nothing, I suppose. I beg your pardon,' he said shortly. 'Your private life is your own affair.' He caught himself up at the *faux pas* and gave her a swift look.

To his surprise, Ginny gave a delighted chuckle. 'Whoops!' Alex's mouth drew into a reluctant grin, and she leaned forward. 'Look, Alex, you're my brother-in-law and I shall always be fond of you, because you made Venetia so happy as well as for old times' sake. But that's as far as it goes. If I'd had any designs on you wouldn't I have come back long before this? If I'd come home immediately after Venetia died I would have slipped into your life without your noticing the difference.' He opened his mouth to make an angry retort, but she waved him into silence. 'Oh, you can protest all you want, but it's true. Why, you even called me Venetia today. Didn't you?'

Reluctantly Alex said, 'Why, yes, but it was only because you'd hurt yourself and I forgot for a moment——'

'Yes, and if I'd come home earlier and made a play for you think how the odd moments could have soon become all the time.' Ginny shook her head, then winced as it hurt. 'Don't get me wrong, Alex; you're a nice guy, but there's no way I want to step into my dead sister's shoes and be called by her name for the rest of my life.'

Reassured at last, Alex visibly relaxed. 'Well, that's a relief. I must admit——'

'You should be so lucky,' Ginny scoffed. 'I came home for my father's funeral, nothing more.'

'But if that's all you came back for, why do you want to keep this house?'

'It's pretty, I like it. And Mother has been on my conscience for some time. I realise that now Venetia's gone I really ought to come over here and see her more often. But just staying with her these last few days has convinced me that I could never share a house with her, so it occurred to me that Bath is just near enough to Cheltenham to be handy, but also far enough away so that I won't be living in Mother's pocket every time I come over.'

Alex smiled. He actually smiled! 'So you intend to make it your English *pied-à-terre*? Why didn't you say so?'

'Frankly, because you've been so darn rude and nasty to me since I got back that I didn't feel like confiding in you.'

He nodded, accepting the rebuke. 'Sorry about that, but you must admit it was natural given the circumstances. I'm glad we've had this talk; it's cleared the air. It was Jeff's idea.'

'Really?' Ginny said drily.

Alex grinned at her tone. 'I've an idea that Jeff's feelings about *you* haven't changed in all these years.'

'In that case he's only in love with a memory, because I've changed completely.'

'Yes, you have,' he agreed contemplatively, adding, 'You don't care for him?'

'I'm afraid I never have.'

Remembering why she hadn't cared for Jeff, Alex gave a deprecatory shrug. 'Yes. Well. That's a shame.' He stood up. 'I'd better be going.'

'Where shall I send the bed?' Ginny asked.

'The bed?' He looked at it through the open doorway of the bedroom, hesitated, then said, 'You keep it. I've sent the stuff I took away to an auction sale. I don't have anywhere to store the bed and I can't see myself ever needing it again. So, yes, you keep it, but thanks all the same.' He looked at her as Ginny got to her feet. 'Are you all right? You look a bit pale.'

'It's just the headache. But perhaps you wouldn't mind bringing my luggage in from the car for me?'

'Yes, of course.' Alex did so, his step lighter than she remembered. 'Well, goodbye, then.' He stood on the top step and held his hand out to her.

'Goodbye, Alex.' Ginny put her left hand in his right and leaned forward to kiss him lightly on the cheek. 'If you want to come back here at any time, you know you're always welcome.'

'Thanks. I appreciate the offer—but I don't think I'll be coming back.'

She nodded, and he turned and walked briskly away. Ginny stood on the step and watched him go, marvelling at how a whole load of lies could so easily defuse a very sensitive situation.

CHAPTER THREE

DISREGARDING her headache, Ginny changed into jeans and a sweater, tied a scarf over her hair and set to work on the house, starting with the sitting-room and bedroom. It was hard work but she welcomed it, glad to have something physical to concentrate on. The trouble was that she kept coming across things that reminded her of Venetia: a scrap-book of Press cuttings, a knitting-basket with a baby's tiny jacket half done. Tears pricked her eyes when she saw the latter, but Ginny ruthlessly threw the knitting into a rubbish bag, along with magazines and newspapers that were two years out of date. The life of the house had stopped at Venetia's death, she realised, when Alex had been unable to bear the memories.

Ginny vacuumed, dusted and polished, making sure she was extremely tired when she at length went to bed, a bed that she had fitted with clean sheets and duvet cover. It felt strange to lie in it, to look at the rays of moonlight lighting the room. Trying very hard not to think of Alex and Venetia making love in this bed, Ginny instead planned the tasks she would do the following day. She must do the kitchen next, she decided, so that she could get in a store of food and cook for herself. Today she had managed with a Chinese meal she had bought on her way back from taking all the curtains in the house to the cleaners.

That was why the moonlight was shining into the room and giving it such a silvery, ghost-like aura.

Her sister's presence felt very close. Ginny hadn't gone into the room on the other side of the landing that Venetia had been making into a nursery. She wasn't afraid of her sister's spirit, in fact gained comfort from being close to her, but she still wasn't sure whether Venetia wanted her here in this house or not.

Ginny's head throbbed and she couldn't sleep. After a couple of hours of restless turning she got up and went into the bathroom to try and find some pain-killers. It was as she was searching through the bathroom cabinet that she became aware of the tapping noise. It was a hollow, echoing sound. For a few seconds Ginny was filled with gut primeval fear, her flesh cringed and she could feel the hair on the back of her neck start to rise. But then the tapping noise defined itself into the drip of water against something metal and Ginny gave a great gasp of relief, gripping the hand basin for a moment to steady her frayed nerves.

It was the water tank that had started to leak and was dripping on to a connecting pipe before enlarging the growing puddle on the attic floor. Ginny went down to the laundry-room in the basement to turn off the stopcock, then turned on all the taps to drain off the system, carefully hoarding some in bowls and buckets so that she would have some water for the morning. She then mopped up the puddle as best she could and switched on an electric fire to try and dry out the attic. After all that, when she finally got back into bed again she fell straight into a deep, exhausted sleep.

There was a telephone in the house but it wasn't connected. After washing in cold water, Ginny sat down and wrote out a list of priorities, the first being to have the phone reconnected. Leaving the house early, she came out just as her next-door neighbour, a well-rounded woman wearing a pink housecoat, was collecting the milk from her doorstep. The woman glanced across—and promptly dropped a bottle of milk, her face ashen. 'V-Venetia!'

'It's OK.' Ginny ran over to her. 'I'm Venetia's sister.'

'God, you gave me a fright.' The woman put a hand over her heart and stared at her. 'You're exactly like her.'

'Yes. We're—we were identical twins.' Ginny glanced down at the broken glass all mixed up with the flowing white liquid. 'I'm sorry about the milk. Can I help you clear it up?'

The woman dragged her eyes away from Ginny's face. 'What? Oh, no. No, I'll do it. I just can't get over...' She pulled herself together. 'I'm Clare Kennedy.'

'Ginny Barclay.' Ginny held out her hand and the other woman shook it, her own still trembling a little.

'I'm glad to feel you're flesh and blood and not a ghost,' Clare said with some relief. 'Oh, I beg your pardon; Venetia was your sister. I remember her talking about you now. You're a model, aren't you? And don't you live in America?'

'That's right,' Ginny acknowledged. 'You seem to have known Alex and Venetia well.'

'Oh, yes, we were neighbours all the time they lived here. We keep an eye on the house for Alex and he usually pops in whenever he's over here.' She gave Ginny a speculative look. 'Have you moved in next door? Alex rang to say that it might be changing hands, but when I heard someone moving around yesterday I thought that Alex was having it cleaned prior to letting or selling it.'

'Yes, I've moved in. For a time at least, but I'm not sure how long I'll be staying.'

'Why don't you come in and have a cup of coffee?' Clare offered.

'Thanks, but I'll have to take a rain-check; I have so much to do today. Can I get you some more milk while I'm doing my shopping?'

'That would be kind of you. Thanks.'

Going first to the post office, Ginny arranged to have the phone reconnected, but, after filling in all the necessary forms, was told it might take at least a week. So she stood in a phone-box, going through the list of plumbers in the Yellow Pages business directory, but unable to find one who could replace the tank immediately. This is England, not America, she reminded herself; be patient. She tried several more, pleading her case, but the earliest any would do the job was in two weeks' time. I can't be without water for two weeks! It's ridiculous, she thought angrily. Ginny hesitated, then picked up the phone again and rang Bristol University. This time she was luckier and caught Alex between seminars.

'Alex, it's Ginny. I'm sorry to trouble you but the water tank started to leak last night and——'

'Have you turned off the water and drained the system?' he interrupted.

'Yes. But I can't get hold of a plumber to put in a new one.'

'Who have you tried?'

'Do you want the whole list? I've spent nearly all my English money in this phone-booth. Plumbers in New York are like gold dust—in Bath they're like platinum,' she said indignantly.

His voice sounding amused, Alex said, 'Leave it to me. I'll try and arrange something.'

'But how will you let me know? It may take British Telecom a week to reconnect the phone.'

She heard him hesitate, then say, 'Don't worry, I'll get a message to you. Will you be in this evening?'

'Oh, sure. Cold, thirsty and unwashed, but I'll be there.'

He gave a short laugh, almost a reluctant sound, and put the phone down without telling her what he was going to do.

After going to a bank to change some dollars into sterling, Ginny did the rest of her shopping, including several heavy bottles of mineral water, and at the last minute remembered her neighbour's replacement bottle of milk. When she got home Ginny put the bottle on Clare Kennedy's newly cleaned step, leaving it there for her to find, then went into her own house to change into jeans again and start work on the kitchen. She was halfway through when the doorbell rang. Hoping that Alex might have found a plumber for her, Ginny ran to open it. But it was Clare Kennedy.

'Hello, I've brought you a welcome cake; isn't that what they do in America?'

They didn't in the circle Ginny had moved in, but she was too polite to say so. 'Why, that's marvellous. Thanks. Won't you come in?'

It was what Clare was obviously hoping for, and she immediately accepted, her eyes going everywhere.

'I'm just cleaning out the kitchen. Would you like a coffee?'

'Love one, please.'

Ginny gestured towards the sitting-room and Clare looked in there but then followed Ginny down to the kitchen. 'I often used to come in here and have coffee with Venetia. Or else we'd sit in the garden in the summer. Hers used to be really pretty, always full of flowers. Ours is always full of the kids' toys and bikes.'

'You have children?'

'Yes. Two. One of each.' She gave Ginny a speculative look. 'Venetia often used to baby-sit for us.'

Not wanting to be tied down at the moment, Ginny didn't rise to the bait. 'You were friends, then?'

'Oh, yes, we used to help each other out. We were both self-employed, you see. Venetia with her modelling classes and me with my cookery.'

'You're a professional cook?'

Clare smiled. 'Taste the cake.'

Ginny did so, and her eyes widened in appreciation. 'It's delicious.'

'Not bad for a home-bakery, is it?'

She began to ask Ginny about her life in New York and Ginny responded readily enough; Clare seemed nice even if she was nosy, and it occurred to Ginny that if her neighbour could keep an eye on the house for Alex then she might do the same for her when she was away.

'You must come over and meet my husband, Richard, and the kids. Tell you what, we're having a small drinks party a week on Saturday. Why don't you come, and then you can meet some of your new neighbours?'

Hoping that Clare hadn't this minute arranged the drinks party in her head so that she could flaunt Ginny as her new celebrity neighbour, Ginny smiled and said, 'Thanks, I'd like to. Is it a special occasion?'

'Oh, no, just something we do now and again,' Clare said airily.

'I just hope my water tank will be repaired by then,' Ginny said ruefully, and they fell into a comfortable chat.

At length Clare remembered that she had cakes in the oven and went home to see to them. Ginny got on with her cleaning as best she could without any water, but no plumbers turned up on her doorstep that afternoon and she began to think that Alex must have had as little luck as she'd had. But around six o'clock the bell rang and she found not a plumber but both Alex and Jeff waiting outside. Jeff had on a decent suit, but Alex was wearing an old, paint-splashed pair of jeans, and she could see a new tank in the back of Jeff's car.

'Hey, that's great.' Ginny ran down the steps to meet them.

'I ordered it from a builder's merchant's and we collected it from the warehouse after work today,' Alex told her. 'But it wouldn't go in my car so we had to bring it in Jeff's.'

'But how about a plumber to fix it?'

'That's me,' Alex said with a crooked grin. 'I'm afraid I'm the best you're going to get if you want it put in today.'

'Oh, I do, *I do*,' Ginny said fervently. 'Hi, Jeff, how are you?' She reached up to kiss him on the cheek, then did the same to Alex in a very sisterly fashion.

The men carried the tank into the house and up to the attic, but then Jeff came down alone. 'I'm afraid I'm giving a talk at a historical society in a village the other side of Bristol tonight so I can't stay and give Alex a hand. I'd like to have done, though.'

'Well, thanks for the thought, and for bringing the tank.' She went up close to him and said in an undertone, 'I know he's a whiz at car engines, but it doesn't necessarily follow that Alex is any good as a plumber. He isn't likely to connect the wrong pipes and blow the place up, is he?'

Jeff laughed aloud. 'I think you'll find he can manage.' He glanced at his watch and said regretfully, 'I'll have to go, unfortunately. I've got to be there by seven-thirty. I'll be over around eleven or so to pick Alex up.'

'Good heavens, no,' Ginny exclaimed. 'There's no point in your coming all the way back here just for that. I'll run him back to Bristol.'

Jeff hesitated, then shrugged. 'All right, thanks. See you some time, then.'

Ginny waved as he drove away, then went up into the attic to find Alex, taking care to keep her head lowered. He was already banging away at the connecting joints on the old metal tank, but paused when he saw her.

'Can I help?'

'How's the head?'

'OK, thanks.'

'Things will be a bit noisy for a while, but I'll be glad of a hand when I put the new tank in place.'

So she left him to it until the hammering stopped, then went up again. 'How's it going?'

'Fine. I've cleaned up all the connections and we'll be able to lift the tank into place shortly to see if it all fits.'

'And if it doesn't?'

'Then I'll have to make some adjustments,' Alex answered, in no way put out. Soon Ginny was being used as a plumber's mate, handing tools and helping to lift the new plastic tank into place. The connections needed some alterations to fit, but instead of going downstairs again Ginny sat on the floor, her legs crossed, and watched as Alex soldered pipes, his hands deft and knowledgeable.

'Almost done,' he told her.

Taking the hint, Ginny went down to the kitchen and ten minutes later took up a tray of coffee and sandwiches for them both.

'I take it you haven't eaten yet?'

'No.' Alex put aside the tool he was using and came over to sit beside her on the floor, wiping his hands on his jeans.

He bit into his sandwich, obviously enjoying it. Ginny took one herself and felt a moment of perfect contentment, sitting here with Alex, working with him. No celebrity-studded gala in New York or

Hollywood could ever compare with this quiet companionship in the dusty attic. All her hard-won success in her job, her fame, couldn't compare with this joy that filled her heart at just being with him.

'You're looking very pensive,' Alex remarked, glancing at her.

'I was thinking about Jeff,' Ginny lied smoothly. 'He seemed really disappointed that he couldn't stay and help you.'

'Yes, he enjoys this kind of thing. I think he likes getting dirty. That's probably why he took up archaeology; so he could have an excuse to grub around in the dirt.'

Ginny smiled. 'He always has seemed like an overgrown schoolboy to me.'

Alex gave her a speculative look. 'That's probably why you don't go for him, then.'

'What do you mean?'

'Well, as you're definitely not the maternal type you obviously wouldn't go for someone you thought of as a schoolboy. Although Jeff is far from that.'

But Ginny had lost all interest in Jeff. 'What makes you think I'm not maternal?' she asked rather indignantly.

Alex gave a short laugh. 'You're a career woman through and through. Anyone can see that. If you'd been interested in a home and family you would have done something about it by now.'

'I'm only twenty-six; I've got loads of time yet.'

'But you wouldn't give up your career. Having children would tie you down, and there's always the possibility that it would spoil your figure.'

There was a slightly sarcastic note in Alex's voice, and Ginny didn't know whether to be annoyed about that or pleased that he'd noticed she had a figure. 'Venetia was willing to have children,' she pointed out.

'But she had settled for a family life, whereas you like to play the field and...' He broke off. 'Sorry. I have no right to criticise you.'

'No, you don't,' Ginny agreed bluntly. 'And anyway, it's perfectly possible for a woman to have a career and a family nowadays.'

'Your kind of career?'

'Why not? Anyway, I'll probably be able to do modelling for another five years at the most; it's a young woman's game and they're always looking for new faces. That's why I'm trying to branch out into acting and television work.'

'And is that why your name is always being coupled with male celebrities'?' Alex asked cynically.

'It helps, yes,' Ginny admitted frankly. 'But you only have to be seen with a man a couple of times and the gossip columns are saying that you're having a hot affair with him.'

'And aren't you?'

Putting down the mug of coffee she was holding, Ginny turned to give Alex a steady look. 'What's it to you, Alex? Why does it make you sound so angry?'

His face tightened. 'To me, nothing, of course. But Venetia was your sister; you might have considered her before you started going with half the famous men in New York.'

'My name was never linked with any man's before Venetia's death,' Ginny answered forcefully. 'You must know that.'

He gave her a frowning look. 'What about that photographer—what was his name?—Blake?'

'You mean Simon Blake. Naturally my name was linked with his; he was my sponsor and then my manager.'

'Was? Isn't he any longer?'

Ginny looked away. 'No, we—agreed to go our separate ways.'

'Maybe he didn't like the life you were leading,' Alex pointed out drily.

Her voice acid, Ginny said, 'Maybe I didn't like the life *he* was leading. You really ought to get your facts right before you start criticising people, Alex. Or is it just that you can't resist trying to hurt me?'

Her attack gave him pause. He looked away and put his hand up to wipe it over his face, leaving a stony mask behind; a gesture she was beginning to recognise. But then he gave a slight shrug. 'I suppose I've been hating you ever since you didn't turn up at Venetia's funeral. Two years is a long time. It's become a habit.' He turned to look at her. 'And I still can't buy what you said about sharing what she went through.'

'Why not? We always shared each other's deep emotions. That's why Venetia knew that I'd been to bed with someone that night I spent with you.' Alex's face tightened, and she knew that it had been a mistake to remind him of their one night of love, so she quickly went on, 'Didn't you go through agony when you heard that Venetia had been hurt? Weren't you almost physically ill with grief when she died?'

'Yes, but that was a natural reaction. You tried to convince me that you had—what would you call it?—an extra-sensory experience.'

Ginny looked away. She rested her chin on her bent knees and gazed at the wall of the attic, her thoughts going back. 'I was on a skiing holiday when it happened,' she said in a low voice. 'I was just about to set off down a steep *piste* when I felt this sudden great, paralysing fear. I've never been so afraid in all my life. I wanted to scream but I couldn't. There wasn't time before—before a terrible pain hit me in the side and then in my head.' Alex's head jerked up at that and he studied her intently, but Ginny didn't look at him before going on. 'Everything went black then, and it was some time before I came round. When I did they told me that I'd fainted and rolled part way down the ski slope. They said that was why I'd felt the pain, but I knew that it had been before—so I knew that something terrible had happened to Venetia.'

She paused, her mouth dry, and licked her lips before she said, 'They—the doctors couldn't understand why I was in such distress when there was nothing outwardly wrong with me except a few bruises. But I made Simon phone my mother and she told us what had happened.'

'You were on holiday with Simon Blake?'

She glanced at him for a brief moment. 'Yes.' Pensive again, Ginny said, 'Mother said that Venetia was still alive, that I should get over as soon as I could, but I knew it wouldn't be any use; I knew she was dying. So I tried to send my spirit to her, to let her know that I was sharing the pain with her, sharing as we had always done. And she knew, she knew I was there.'

'You only say that to comfort yourself,' Alex cut in sharply. 'You can't possibly know.'

'No?' Ginny turned her head to look at him. 'Then how come that it was my name that she spoke just as she died?'

Alex stared, his face suddenly grey. 'How can you possibly know that? I was alone with her when she died.'

Ginny gave him a steady but sad look, then picked up their empty mugs and plates without adding anything further. He either believed her or he didn't; there was nothing more she could say that would convince him now.

'Let me know when you want the stopcock turned on.'

'What?' Alex gave her a rather dazed look. 'Oh, yes, OK. Shouldn't be long now.'

Ginny carried the tray downstairs but almost half an hour had passed before Alex yelled down to her. The water gushed through the pipes as it had done yesterday and she ran back upstairs. 'Is it OK? No leaks?'

'Give it time to fill.' But his voice was back to normal and, after a sneaking look at his face, Ginny was relieved to see that the grim look had left his mouth. She gave an inner sigh of relief; maybe he would never be able to completely understand the closeness of the bond there had been between her and her twin, but at least he had opened his mind and wasn't so hostile now.

After assuring himself that the tank wasn't leaking, Alex went round the house, checking that there weren't any air-locks in the radiators. 'You've certainly cleaned the place up,' he remarked grudgingly.

'Thank you,' Ginny returned lightly. 'I expect you'd like a shower. I've put some clean towels in the bathroom.'

Alex gave her a rather sardonic look at being told what to do, but he went anyway, rejoining her about twenty minutes later with his hair still damp.

'I've made some more coffee; the proper stuff this time, as we have fresh water now.' Alex looked as if he was going to refuse, so Ginny added quickly, 'And there's some cake your neighbour brought round today.'

'Clare?' Alex gave a wry grin. 'I imagine she was surprised to see you.'

'She thought she'd seen a ghost,' Ginny agreed with a smile. 'I imagine it will be the talk of the neighbourhood.'

'She's OK, but she's a bit of a gossip. I suppose she was asking you all sorts of questions. What did you tell her?' he asked reluctantly.

'All that she wanted to know—about my glamorous life in New York,' Ginny added, after a deliberate pause. 'And that was all I told her.'

Alex nodded. He bit into the cake and ate it, then grinned, 'Maybe this was what Jeff was so disappointed about; he could never resist Clare's cakes.'

'Nor can you, by the look of it. You'd better take the rest of it back with you.'

'How about you?'

'I'm a model, remember,' Ginny said with a laugh. 'But trust me to end up living next to a woman who can cook cakes like that. I shall probably put on pounds.'

She pulled a doleful face as she spoke and Alex gave a crack of laughter, then looked surprised, as if he hadn't laughed for a long time. He became a little withdrawn after that, and, as soon as he'd finished his coffee, stood up. 'I'd better get going.'

Making no attempt to get him to stay longer, Ginny found a box for the cake while Alex collected up the tools he'd brought with him. 'How much do I owe you for the tank?' she asked.

He shook his head. 'If the house had still been mine I would have replaced the tank with a new one anyway.'

'Oh, but I can't let you do that, Alex.'

'I've said no,' he told her brusquely, turning away. 'Let's go, shall we?'

Ginny got her jacket and drove to Bristol, Alex giving her directions to the building on the university campus where he had his rooms. He didn't ask her in.

'Thanks for the tank and for giving up your time,' Ginny said warmly. 'I'm very grateful.'

'It's OK.' Alex reached for the door-handle, then paused. 'Ginny, I know this was an exception, but I really feel that it would be better if we didn't meet again.'

Her hands tightened on the wheel. 'You mean—not ever?' she asked, striving to keep any emotion out of her voice.

'That's right. We've both got our own lives to lead, and they're so vastly different that I really feel that we have nothing in common now, so paying duty calls whenever you happened to be in England would just be a waste of time.' He must have already worked all this out in his mind. Alex spoke as if it was the most common-sense decision in the world, but there was a tightness in his voice that he couldn't quite hide.

'I see.' Ginny took a deep breath. 'But what if I decide to sell you the house eventually?'

'I'm sure our solicitors could handle that perfectly well.'

'Yes, of course.' She turned to face him, her chin up but her hands gripping the steering-wheel. 'This is—goodbye, then?'

'Yes.' Alex hesitated, groping for words, then said shortly, 'I hope all goes well for you, Ginny. That you—get what you want out of life.'

She nodded and her face tightened. He went to get out of the car but she called sharply, 'Alex.'

He turned back with evident reluctance. 'Yes?'

'Don't forget your cake.'

He got out and Ginny sped away, deliberately forcing herself not to look back. She had looked back so many times in the past and there had never been anything there but sadness. She wouldn't look now, *she wouldn't*. What was one more heartbreak to add to the rest?

When she got back home Ginny ran a bath and lay in it until the water cooled. Looking back on the evening, it occurred to her that it was her mention of the night she had spent with him that might have made Alex decide that he didn't want to ever see her again.

But then it might not have been that, it could have been seeing the house looking clean and homely again. Anything. Putting on her nightdress, Ginny lay in bed and looked at the clean patch on the wall over the fireplace where Venetia's studio portrait had been. Alex had taken that away when the furniture went. I must have this room redecorated, she thought. In fact, I think I'll have the whole house done. It will give me something else to think about. Or I can go back to New York and resume my career. But somehow that lifestyle had lost a great deal of its attraction now.

It seemed that decorators in Bath were as hard to get hold of as plumbers. After spending another small fortune in a public phone-booth, Ginny gave up and bought several tins of paint instead. She and Venetia had done some decorating before, when they'd had their old flat in East Finchley. Now it seemed strange to be working alone at first, but Ginny turned on the radio to shut out the memories and was soon enjoying herself.

When Jeff called round a couple of afternoons later he found Ginny trying to paint the ceiling in the sitting-room, using a board suspended on a chair at one end and on a rung of a step-ladder at the other.

'Hi. Come on in,' she greeted him. 'As you can see, I'm up to my eyes in paint. Literally,' she added with a laugh, as she wiped a drip of paint from her forehead.

'I didn't expect to find you doing this kind of thing,' Jeff remarked in surprise.

'No? What did you expect to find, then?'

He pushed his glasses up his nose. 'Well, I happened to ask Alex if he was going to call round to see that the water tank was still functioning. And he said...' He hesitated.

'That he didn't intend to come here again,' Ginny finished for him.

'Yes. So I thought I'd just call in and make sure you were all right.'

'I suppose you thought I'd be moping around feeling sorry for myself, did you?' It wasn't very hard to give him an amused look. 'I told you; I was over Alex years ago. If he doesn't want to come to the house while I'm here, it's perfectly understandable.'

'That wasn't quite what he said.'

'You mean he said that he didn't want to see *me* ever again. Well, that's understandable, too. It can't be very pleasant to have someone around who looks exactly like the woman you loved.' Turning away, she climbed back on to the board and dipped her brush in the tin of paint. 'And maybe it will be a good thing if Alex stays away. Now that he's got rid of this house there's nothing to bring him back and he might start to get his life back together again.'

'You're a good loser, Ginny,' Jeff said sincerely.

She gave a bitter little laugh and hit the brush hard against the ceiling, sending a spray of splashes over the old clothes she was wearing. 'Oh, sure.'

'Would you like some help with that?'

Ginny glanced down at him. At the moment she wished that Jeff hadn't come; all he'd done was to revive feelings that she'd been trying hard to conquer and now had to try even harder to hide from him. But he had done so from the kindest of intentions. So Ginny stifled a sharp retort and instead gave him a grateful smile. 'Of course. Especially someone with arms as long as yours. But what about your clothes? They'll get ruined.'

'I've got some old things in the car that I keep for when I visit a dig.'

'Great. In that case you can definitely take over the ceiling while I start on the walls.'

They worked companionably, talking a little, mostly concentrating on the painting, and got a lot done before they called it a day and went out to find a restaurant for dinner. Jeff came again the next afternoon and offered to help at the weekend, but Ginny resolutely told him that she was going over to her mother's place for both days. But he turned up early on Monday afternoon and they started work on the hall and landing, a difficult job requiring ladders and scaffold boards that Ginny wouldn't have contemplated doing on her own.

Clare Kennedy just happened to drop in while Jeff was there, but they had known each other when Venetia was alive so were pleased to see each other again. And Jeff bought two rich cream cakes from her to take back to his rooms. That week Ginny left the difficult jobs for Jeff and worked on the bathroom and the kitchen during the days, the latter being easy as there wasn't much bare wall left to paint. By Thursday evening they were finished and able to stand back and contemplate their handiwork with some pride.

'What about the other bedroom?' Jeff asked her. 'It wouldn't take me long to do that.'

But Ginny shook her head. 'I haven't decided what I'm going to do with that yet.' She turned to him and gave an affectionate smile. Jeff's old jeans, already torn in a couple of places, were now liberally splashed with paint, mostly white, giving him a leopard-like effect. His hair, too, looked as if he had suddenly and prematurely aged. 'Are you doing anything tomorrow?' she asked him.

'Why? What would you like me to do?' He was all willing eagerness.

'I'd like you to get rid of all that paint, dress yourself up in your best evening suit, and let me take you out to dinner as a thank-you for all your help this past week.'

'That isn't necessary. I've enjoyed it.'

But Ginny had her way, and the next evening she drove over to Bristol to pick him up. It was a bright evening and not yet dark when she arrived on the campus. Ginny got out of the car to go and knock for him, but Jeff opened the window of his rooms and called out that he would be right down. She nodded and waved, a tall, very slim figure in a long, halter-necked cream dress that hugged her figure and accentuated the California tan that hadn't yet faded in the English spring. As Jeff drew back in and shut the window, Ginny's eye was caught by a movement at a window a little further along. Intuitively she knew that it was Alex. Ginny didn't attempt to wave, but she didn't get back into the car until Jeff joined her, looking handsome but slightly uncomfortable in his dress suit.

Making the most of the occasion, he put his arm round her waist and kissed her cheek. 'Where are we going?' he asked as they got into the car.

Driving away from the university, Ginny said, 'Well, there's this really quaint little fish and chip shop I've found where they do the most delicious pease pudding and faggots...' And then burst into laughter at the comical look of dismay on Jeff's face.

She took him to London, zipping up the motorway. They ate in a four-star restaurant and afterwards went on to a nightclub to dance and then a casino to play the tables. 'Phew! Do you always live like this?' Jeff demanded at four o'clock in the morning when they walked to the car to drive home.

'There was a time,' Ginny admitted. 'But then the high life began to show and I realised that if I went on with it I'd have to give up modelling, so I went back to early nights and sobriety.'

'Let me drive,' Jeff offered when they reached the car, but Ginny shook her head and got into the driving-seat. She did it automatically, but then realised that if it had been Alex she would have let him drive, not because he was a better driver than Jeff but because he wouldn't have asked, he would have just got into the driving-seat and taken over. She could dominate Jeff, but Alex couldn't be dominated unless he wanted to be.

During all the evenings she and Jeff had worked together on the house, Alex's name had hardly been mentioned—they certainly hadn't discussed him—but the thought of him filled her mind now as Ginny drove back to Bristol through the dark night. Jeff half lay in the seat beside her, slumped into it, his head against the rest, dozing a little. But it was as if he guessed her thoughts, because he presently said, 'Alex may have given up all rights to your house, but he hasn't lost interest in it. He keeps asking me how we're getting on, what changes you're making. That kind of thing.'

'Really?' Ginny was careful to keep the word casual.

'Yes. I told him that you were just repainting, of course.' Jeff, relaxed by the food and wine he'd had that evening, gave a short laugh. 'I've an idea Alex thinks we may be getting friendly again. He always seems to be around when I get home lately.'

'He'll have had a long wait up tonight, then,' Ginny said drily, making Jeff laugh.

'He'll wonder what's happened.' Jeff looked at her, and then sighed. 'I suppose nothing is going to happen, is it?' And then answered his own question. 'No, of course not. We both knew that from the start.'

'I'm sorry, Jeff.' She took her hand from the wheel momentarily and touched his.

'Will you let me take *you* out tomorrow—or rather later today?'

'I'm afraid I already have a date.' He gave her a questioning glance but she didn't enlighten him, saying instead, 'But you're welcome at any time, you know that. Why don't you come round one night next week and I'll cook dinner for you?'

They lapsed into silence and hardly spoke again until they got back to Bristol. As Jeff said goodnight and got out, Ginny glanced up at Alex's windows. They were in darkness, as you'd have expected them to be, but she noticed that the curtains were open. If he was lying awake he would have seen the flash of the headlights as they drove up. If he was awake. If he cared. But he had been asking Jeff what they were doing. Although, with her kind of luck, it most probably was just the house that Alex was interested in.

Ginny dressed carefully for Clare Kennedy's party the next evening. To be 'New York' glamorous would be going over the top for just a small gathering, but to be too casual might be construed as looking down on her hostess. In the end Ginny chose a pair of deep red silk evening trousers with a matching sleeveless top, and used a bandanna in the same colour to tie back her long, luxuriant hair. Her toenails she had already painted in a pretty, paler shade of red and they looked good when she put a pair of strap sandals on her bare feet. She had rested most of that day and her face looked OK, but any lasting signs of tiredness had been skilfully covered by make-up. Ginny added perfume—her favourite, Joy—and glanced at her watch.

Eight-forty. Clare had said around eight but Ginny had no intention of being the first to arrive; in her profession you learned how to make an entrance. Getting ready in her bedroom with the window partly open, she had heard Clare's front door being opened and closed several times, making her wonder just how small this party was going to be. Picking up her bag, Ginny ran downstairs to pick up the bottle of wine she'd bought to take with her, made sure the house was securely locked, and walked the few yards to the next door along.

A man came in answer to her ring. 'Hello, there. You must be Ginny Barclay.' An average kind of man in his mid-thirties with the start of a paunch, his eyes went over her appreciatively.

'And you must be Richard Kennedy.'

'That's right.' He was obviously pleased that she'd remembered his name. 'Do come in. We're so glad you could make it.'

'I wouldn't have missed it,' Ginny assured him, and held out the bottle. 'My contribution.'

'Oh, really, you shouldn't have bothered. But thanks anyway.' He put the bottle down on the hall table. 'Let me hand you over to Clare, and then I'll get you a drink.'

Opening the door of the sitting-room, he was met by the sort of noise people made at the beginning of a party, when they were still feeling each other out and hadn't yet had enough to drink to laugh a lot and get loud, certainly not yet loud enough to drown the music that was playing in the background. But there were at least twenty people there, Ginny guessed as he ushered her in.

'Clare,' Richard said into the silence that fell as they all turned to look at her. 'Here's Ginny. What would you like to drink?' he asked as his wife came over.

'White wine, please.'

'Hello, Ginny. Come and meet everyone. These are your neighbours on the other side.' Clare gave Ginny a social kiss on the cheek, then took her round the room, introducing her. Ginny smiled and said hello, but hardly took in any of the names. Her eyes had only flicked over him for a brief second, but she was aware of a man standing alone in the far corner of the room near the window, a tall man with a drink in his hand. He was the last person whom Clare took her to meet, but then she laughed in obvious self-congratulation and said, 'Now here's someone I don't have to introduce you to, do I? We decided to give you a surprise, Ginny. We thought you'd enjoy yourself more if there was someone here you knew, so we invited him along. Oh, excuse me, there's the doorbell again.'

Clare went away, leaving them suddenly alone in that crowded room, and Ginny licked her tongue over lips gone strangely dry before saying, 'Hello, Alex.'

CHAPTER FOUR

He had had time to get over the initial shock but there was still a trace of tension in Alex's voice as he returned her greeting. 'Hello, Ginny.'

For once she couldn't think of anything to say, but luckily Richard Kennedy came up with her glass of wine and stayed to chat for a few minutes until Clare called him to get someone else a drink and he left them alone again.

'I didn't expect you to be here,' Alex said shortly. 'Jeff said you had a date for tonight.'

So he'd checked. 'This was it,' Ginny replied inadequately.

She took a sip of the wine and half turned away from him, looking round the room. Immediately she was aware of being watched. This wasn't exactly unusual for her, but Ginny realised that tonight it was for a different reason; most of the people there were neighbours and had known Alex and Venetia when they lived next door, so to see Ginny with Alex must surely have aroused their curiosity.

'Does Clare go in for this kind of thing often?' she asked Alex.

'Drinks parties? Probably about a couple of times a year.'

'No, I meant springing this kind of surprise on people.'

'Oh, that.' Alex gave a short laugh. 'I suppose she had no reason to think that we wouldn't both be pleased by it.' He paused, as if debating whether to say something, and then jerked out, 'Jeff tells me you were trying to redecorate the house yourself.'

'Yes, I couldn't get hold of a decorator who would give me a definite starting date.'

'But you've finished it now?'

'With a great deal of help from Jeff, yes.'

'You should have asked me; I could have recommended a good decorator that we always used.'

Ginny sipped her wine, not bothering to state the obvious. Some more people had arrived and the room was too full; it was getting hot and smoky. The doors to the dining-room were closed, which didn't help. Clare was coming over to them, bringing a couple to be introduced. Ginny had started to smile at her when Alex said, 'I'd like to see what you've done to the house. That's if you don't mind, of course.'

She gave him an amazed look but had to turn away to shake hands with the new arrivals and listen to Clare giving them a run-down on who she was and her relationship to Alex. 'A model,' they exclaimed. 'And your wife's twin sister, how amazing.'

By the time they moved away Ginny's smile was fixed and strained and Alex looked quite grim. 'I'm getting tired of this,' he said tensely. 'I shouldn't have come.'

'Why did you, then?'

The question took him by surprise, and she had the feeling that it had momentarily disconcerted him. 'Clare and Richard are friends,' he answered after a moment. 'They were very good to me after—when I needed them.'

'That's no reason for coming when you didn't want to.'

'Maybe it's time I got out and met people again; I'm always being told so.'

'If you don't feel it yourself there isn't much point, though. It's a mistake to try and force yourself.'

Alex turned to study her face. 'You speak as if you had experience.'

'Do I?' She was watching Clare open the doors into the dining-room and call out that the food was ready. 'Good, I'm hungry.' Ginny turned to Alex. 'Would you get me another drink? It's white wine.'

When Alex came back with her drink Ginny had a plate of food and was sitting with a couple of women her own age, chatting quite happily. She took the drink from him with a murmured word of thanks but immediately turned to listen to the conversation again. Neither of the women had known Venetia, so it was easy to talk to them. They were unmarried career women who shared a house further along the road. Although they had started out in different jobs, they were now partners in a corporate entertainment business, mainly at big sporting events. Both women were highly motivated and ambitious and keen to sound Ginny out on similar American businesses. It was an area Ginny knew quite well and they were still talking when the music was turned up and everyone started dancing.

Richard Kennedy came over to them. 'Come on, girls,' he said in a joking voice that nevertheless contained a note of disapproval. 'We can't have you dedicated career women talking shop all evening. Who's going to be first to dance with me, then?'

As they were all aware that most of the men in the room had probably been talking business all evening without earning a remonstrance, he was met by cool looks from three pairs of eyes, and no volunteer to dance with him. So he reached down and took Ginny's hand, pulling her to her feet.

'And what do you do for a living, Richard?' she asked him, as they began to smooch round the room.

'Actually, I'm a financial consultant,' he told her, making it sound as if this were some professional pedestal. 'I advise several large local firms as well as some of the wealthier private individuals who live in and around Bath.' He gave her an assessing look. 'Perhaps I could help you if you decide to invest some money in England.'

Ginny gave him a dazzling smile. 'I'm so sorry, you've just said you don't like people talking shop. And you're right—it can be boring, can't it?'

He blinked, not sure whether he was being snubbed or not, but Ginny quickly changed the subject, asking him about his other interests, and he was soon talking enthusiastically again. The record came to an end and Ginny thanked him and moved apart before another tune could start; Richard seemed nice enough but a bit too chauvinistic for her liking. She went over to find her drink, but found that Alex and a man he was talking to were standing in front of the bookshelf where she'd left her glass.

'Excuse me. Can I get my drink?'

His companion stepped aside but Alex didn't move. Ginny glanced at him and surprised a strange, almost fearful look on his face. But then he said roughly, 'Let's dance,' and, without a word of apology to the man he was with, put his hand on her arm to lead her the couple of steps into the centre of the room.

He held her very loosely, a gap between them, but the fact that he was doing so at all held Ginny speechless. She had only ever danced with him once before, when he and Jeff had come to watch her and Venetia do their cabaret act at a company dinner, and they had joined in the dancing afterwards. They hadn't been enemies then; he had treated her as his girlfriend's sister, been amusing and friendly. And it was during that dance that Ginny had realised just how much she loved him, had accepted that Alex would be the one big love of her life. And had then watched him walk away to her sister's side.

And now? Ginny couldn't understand why he'd asked her to dance but she wasn't about to spoil it by saying a word. Afraid that even a look of surprise might alter his mood, she rested her hand lightly in his and looked fixedly over his shoulder. But it seemed even that was wrong, because after a few minutes Alex said in a growly voice, 'Don't you want to dance?'

Ginny raised her eyes to meet his, trying to still the thumping of her heart. 'Why?'

'You always meet a question with a question.' But he added, 'You were chattering away with Richard, yet you might as well be dumb for all you've said to me.'

'I'm afraid of saying the wrong thing,' Ginny admitted honestly. 'And I wasn't really chatting to Richard; I was just listening to him talk.'

A gleam of amusement came into Alex's eyes. 'Telling you how to rearrange your investments, was he?'

'He offered to, but I gathered that he would have to be paid to do that. Only telling me what sports I should take up, what books I should read, and what car I should drive came for free.'

Alex gave a crack of laughter and she felt the arm he had round her relax. 'Venetia didn't like him much either. But she got on well with Clare.'

'Clare's nice,' Ginny agreed warmly, adding pensively, 'Perhaps Richard is jealous of her popularity.'

'Perhaps.' Alex gave a slight shrug of uninterest.

'Jeff tells me you're working on the use of lasers in medicine now. And also that you're a professor. That you have a chair—is that the right expression?—in physics at the university.'

'Jeff talks too much. But I bet he didn't tell you that he's been offered a prestige job at Oxford.'

'No, he didn't. Is he going to take it?'

'He'll be a fool if he doesn't,' Alex said candidly. 'But he's got this damn fool idea in his head that I can't manage without him.'

'Which is why you came tonight,' Ginny said shrewdly.

'You're very acute,' Alex observed, looking down at her. 'But then you always were. Yes, that was one of the reasons,' he went on, glancing away. 'Jeff needs to realise that I don't need a nursemaid.'

'What were your other reasons for coming, if you didn't particularly want to?'

'I don't know. To get away from the usual faculty crowd for once. Perhaps to meet new people.'

'And to see if you could come back—alone?' Ginny hazarded.

'That, too, I suppose. It isn't easy being a man on your own at a party like this.'

'It's worse being a woman,' Ginny said on an unthinkingly acid note.

Alex gave her a swift, intense glance, but then dropped the subject.

It wasn't an easy silence. 'Tell me about your work,' Ginny invited, to break it.

'It would bore you,' he said shortly.

'Does it bore you?'

'No, of course not.' He looked surprised.

'Then why should it bore me? An expert talking on his subject is always interesting.'

Alex's mouth quirked. 'I'm beginning to see how you got Richard to talk while you listened.' He shook his head. 'It isn't a subject to dance to. Maybe I'll tell you some other time.'

He tightened his hold a little so that they were dancing normally, not as if one of them suffered from halitosis, Ginny thought with a sudden inward giggle. She felt elated, excited, because things had somehow changed. Alex had spoken as if they would be seeing each other again in the future. Ginny grabbed hold of that, but was afraid to look past it. But that didn't matter; for now it was enough that she was held in his arms in this crowded, noisy room full of strangers. Enough that she could feel his hand against her back, strong and alive. That his other hand held hers and she only had to raise her eyes to look at his face, to see the leanness of his cheeks, the fullness of his lower lip, and his long-lashed grey eyes. Features that she had remembered and dreamt about for so long, and had never expected to actually see again.

The music ended, and she expected him to nod and walk away, but it was followed by another slow number and he danced on. Ginny had to be very careful not to let her feelings show, but it was difficult to stop her hand from trembling or to conceal the sudden tremor of emotion that ran through her when someone pushed against them and their bodies touched momentarily. Only when the music changed to a fast beat some ten minutes later did they move apart. Feeling bemused, Ginny found her drink and was immediately pounced on by one of the two career women, who invited her to have lunch with them the next day. Having nothing better to do, Ginny accepted.

During the next hour or so Ginny had another couple of drinks and moved around the room, talking to a lot of people. She felt relaxed, happy, but the inner excitement was still there and, as time passed, she began to feel expectant, too. Around midnight some young couples who had to get home for baby-sitters started to leave. Ginny glanced across at Alex, and it was as if she'd given him the discreet signal that married couples often used. He gave a slight nod, and after a couple of minutes excused himself from the group he was talking to and came over to her.

'Ready to show me your whitewash job?'

'Did Jeff say it was as bad as that?' Ginny returned lightly, but her heart was thumping crazily again.

'He's a much better archaeologist than he is a painter and decorator. Let's say goodnight to our hosts.'

They did so, ignoring the curious glances they got when they left together. 'You realise we'll be talked about now, don't you?' Ginny said when the door shut behind them.

Alex shrugged. 'They must be hard up for gossip, then.' He took a bunch of keys from his pocket and unlocked the door of her house as if he still owned it. Ginny said nothing about his not having given back all the keys, not sure whether she was pleased about it or not. Going into the sitting-room first, Alex looked around. Not only was the room repainted, but Ginny had also rearranged the furniture, adding pieces that she'd bought to replace those Alex had taken away, and hung a couple of pictures she had found in a local art gallery.

'It looks a completely different room,' he remarked, his voice sounding quite unemotional, so that she couldn't tell how he felt about it.

He wandered round the rest of the house, but Ginny didn't go with him, instead going down to the kitchen to make coffee and then carrying it upstairs to the sitting-room where Alex rejoined her.

'You haven't redecorated the spare bedroom,' he said bluntly.

'No.'

'Any special reason?' He took the cup of coffee she held out to him and went to sit in an armchair.

'I don't anticipate using it,' Ginny said quickly, then hesitated before adding, 'No, that isn't true. The first time I went in that room, when you showed me over the house, I felt Venetia's presence very strongly there. I haven't been into it since.'

Alex's eyes widened. 'I felt nothing when I went in there. I never have.'

'Maybe it isn't there any more. But I guess I'll leave the room as it is, just in case.'

He gave her an odd look. 'I didn't think something like that would stop you. When Jeff told me about the redecorating I thought you were trying to drive Venetia's memory out of the house. And perhaps mine, too,' he added deliberately.

'I have no reason to want to forget Venetia,' Ginny replied evenly. 'Or you.'

Alex gave her a long, considering look and set his cup aside. Leaning forward, he put his hands together, intertwining the fingers, looking down at them. 'I haven't been very nice to you since you came back to England,' he said, the curtness in his tone robbing it of apology. 'I've been thinking about it this last couple of weeks and I've come to the conclusion that it's because I've always felt guilty about you.'

'Guilty?' Ginny faltered.

'Yes. I knew that both you and Venetia were in love with me; you told me so that last day before you left. But I was hopelessly confused by finding out what had happened. Venetia said once that I was in love with both of you without realising it, and I think she was right. I ought to have broken with both of you, of course, but I didn't. I let Venetia back into my life—because I couldn't resist her, quite frankly. And because you had gone away and never attempted to get in touch, it was easy to go on almost as if nothing had happened, to get married and to live our lives as if you had never existed.' He raised his eyes to see her reaction. 'I tried to shut you out completely—and I largely succeeded.'

He continued to look at her, but Ginny merely nodded silently, not wanting to interrupt him.

'But there were times,' Alex went on, his hands tightening so that the knuckles showed white, 'when I couldn't shut you out. When Venetia stood with the sunlight behind her I remembered how you had stood, completely naked and very beautiful, on the morning after the night we spent together. And there were other things, little things, that often made me think of you. And it was then that I would feel so guilty. You had given yourself to me so freely, so generously, that night. It was the most wonderful night of my life, then and after.' Ginny gave a small exclamation, her eyes wide and vulnerable, and Alex answered her unspoken question. 'Yes, it's true. But I came to feel that I had driven you away. There were times when I even felt that your going with so many men was in some way my fault. That you were doing it out of anger—and perhaps revenge.'

Ginny gave him a long look, her heart beating with gladness to know that he had thought of her during the long years of separation, that he still thought of that night as she did, with such wonderful memories. But it troubled her that he'd had, and presumably still had, guilt feelings about her. She didn't want that. If there was ever to be a future for them she didn't want it to be based on anything but love. Her mind racing, she said slowly, 'I'm glad you remember that night; it was special for me, too. But why should you feel guilty? You couldn't have married both of us. As it was, you made Venetia very happy.'

'I hope so; she had such a short time, my poor darling. And sometimes I used to feel guilty because I'd thought of you when I was with her.' He laughed harshly, 'Crazy, wasn't it? I just couldn't win, no matter how much I tried to shut you out of my thoughts.' He put his hands up to his face. 'When she was killed I went to pieces for a while. And in a way I was glad that you didn't come to the funeral. It made me feel that all the guilt feelings I'd had about you were unjustified, and that you were just a jealous little trouble-making cat we'd been well rid of. I had to hate something or someone, and it became easy to hate you when you never wrote or got in touch.'

'When I was well enough to write it seemed too late; that anything I said would have been inadequate.'

'You were right; it would have been,' Alex agreed. He sighed deeply. 'When I saw you at your father's funeral I felt such fury, such pure rage. I thought I'd learnt to control myself, and I think for the past eighteen months or so I've been more or less numb, just going through the motions of living. But my feelings that day took me by surprise. I wanted to hit out at you, because I thought you'd put your career before Venetia, and because you looked so exactly like her that you brought her loss so painfully back again.' He paused, then added deliberately, 'And most of all, I suppose, because your coming back would mean that I'd have to face up to the way I used to feel about you. And I didn't want that. That's why I said that I didn't want us ever to meet again. I wanted to go back to being a zombie. Not having any feelings was safe. If you had no feelings you couldn't be hurt again.'

'But now?' Ginny prompted.

He shrugged. 'During the last couple of weeks I tried to shut you out and go back to where I was, but it was impossible, of course. Once shaken out of my apathy, I found there was no going back. And Jeff didn't help by coming back every night and reporting on what you'd been doing to the house.' He glanced at her. 'That night you took him up to town, I thought he was going to spend the night with you. I'm ashamed to say that I didn't like the idea at all.'

Ginny's heart lurched and she had to lower her head to hide the sudden radiance that lit her eyes. 'Why not?'

'I still felt a proprietorial interest in you, I suppose. Stupid as it seems, that one night we spent together makes me feel—possessive. Even seeing your name linked with other men couldn't kill that.'

'And have you stopped feeling guilty now?' Ginny asked lightly. 'You have no need to be, you know.'

'But what about you? You not only walked away from me but you lost Venetia, too. You just cut yourself off completely.'

It seemed that he still needed reassurance, so she said, 'That was the general idea. It was what Venetia and I agreed between us.'

'Before you tossed the coin to decide who would stay and who would go?'

She gave him a startled look. 'Venetia told you about that?'

Alex shook his head and gave a wry smile. 'No, she always kept that a secret.'

'How, then?'

'I was watching you from the window of the hotel room. I knew you always settled things between you by tossing a coin, so it wasn't hard to guess what you were deciding that day.'

'We both thought you'd be furious if you ever found out.'

'I was at first, but thank goodness I had enough sense to know that my life would have been completely empty without—one of you.' His eyes went to her face.

'You mean without Venetia,' Ginny corrected him firmly. 'And if it comes to guilt, I had my share of that, too. I should have backed off when I found that you and Venetia were going out together. And I should never have pretended to be her that night.' But, even as she said it, the thought filled her mind that if Venetia hadn't deceived Alex into thinking it was her he'd met originally instead of Ginny, how different their lives would have been. She gave an angry shake of her head and stood up. 'What's the point of thinking about the past?' she said irritably. 'You can't change it, so you might as well forget it.'

'Is that what you do—live from day to day?'

Ginny gave a small laugh. 'What other way is there?'

'That sounds—very disillusioned.'

'Does it?' Going over to the window, Ginny closed the curtains, shutting out a little more noise from the party that was still going on next door. Then she turned to face him and said firmly, 'You weren't responsible for what happened to me, Alex. If you hadn't come along I would still have gone to America and become a model. Venetia and I would have gone our separate ways. My life wouldn't have been any different than it is now.'

'No?' The implication was obvious; he was thinking about the men her name had been linked with in the last two years.

'No,' Ginny answered firmly. 'What happened between us was a long, long time ago, Alex. Actually, I got over my—my feelings for you pretty quickly. I had to, because there was no point in brooding over it. And I enjoyed my work and my new life. Although I missed Venetia incredibly, of course.'

'And after she died; was it then you started going with men?' Alex asked, his voice grim.

'Let's set the record straight, Alex; I didn't *go* with men, not in the sense you mean. I was *seen* with them, which is an entirely different thing. And no, Venetia's death wasn't the cause of it.' She hesitated, then gave a small inward sigh, realising that there was no point in holding anything back. 'I started dating other men a few months after Venetia died because that happened to be when I was free to do so. It was then that—that my divorce came through.'

Alex's head jerked up and he stared at her in stunned disbelief. 'Your divorce! Do you mean to say that you were *married*?'

'I believe it is compulsory to be married before you can get a divorce,' Ginny agreed with a flicker of wry amusement.

He came to his feet. 'But who to? Did Venetia know? She never said anything to me about any marriage.'

'I don't know whether she knew or not. Mother knew, so I expect she told Venetia, but obviously she thought you'd rather not know.'

His jaw thrusting forward, Alex said angrily, 'She should have told me.'

'Why?' Ginny asked mildly. 'You've said tonight that you were trying to convince yourself that I'd never existed. Venetia must have known that and decided not to take the risk of making you angry.'

'It would have changed things,' he insisted. 'Who did you marry? An American?'

'No.' Ginny shook her head. 'I married Simon Blake, the photographer who got my career going.'

'I thought he was a lot older than you,' Alex said with a frown.

'Almost twenty years older.'

'Is that why it didn't work out?'

'Oh, there were thousands of reasons why it didn't work out. What we could never understand was the reason why we got married in the first place. We spent a couple of years trying to figure it out and then gave up and got a divorce.'

'You sound so—casual about it. I can hardly believe it,' Alex said wonderingly.

Ginny had felt far from casual about it when the marriage had finally broken up, and knew that it had contributed to her nervous breakdown, but there was no need to tell Alex that. 'It was a mistake from the start. We both knew it, although it seemed the right thing to do at the time.'

'Was the divorce very——' Alex sought for the right word '—very acrimonious?'

Four free Romances and two free gifts for you

As an introduction to our Reader Service, we invite you to accept four spell-binding Mills & Boon Romances plus two gifts absolutely FREE.

Romances every month!

At the same time we'll reserve a subscription for you; which means that you could go on to receive SIX BRAND NEW ROMANCES *every month*. What's more, we'll pay for all the postage and packing, and we'll include our free NEWsletter - featuring recipes, author news, horoscopes, competitions, and much more.

And, as an *extra bonus*, when you return this card we'll also send you TWO FREE GIFTS - our own cuddly Teddy Bear plus an intriguing mystery gift.

So you've nothing to lose, whatever you decide, the four free books and two free gifts will be yours to keep - so don't delay, REPLY TODAY!

FREE

**Reader Service
FREEPOST
P.O. Box 236
Croydon
Surrey
CR9 9EL**

Free Romances and gifts

Yes! Please send me four specially selected
Mills & Boon Romances, together with my
FREE Teddy and mystery gift - and reserve a Reader Service
subscription for me. If I decide to subscribe, I will receive six
brand new books each month for just £9.60. If I decide not
to subscribe I shall write to you within 10 days. The FREE
books and gifts are mine to keep in any case. I understand
that I may cancel or suspend my subscription at any time
simply by writing to you. I am over 18 years of age.

11A1R

Signature _____

Ms/Miss/Mrs/Mr _____

Address _____

_____ Postcode _____

Offer expires 31st December 1991. The right is reserved to refuse
an application and change the terms of this offer. Readers overseas
and in Eire please send for details. Southern Africa write to
Independent Book Services, Postbag X3010, Randburg 2125. You
may be mailed with offers from other reputable companies as a
result of this application. If you would prefer not to share in this
opportunity, please tick box. ☐

Going over to the sideboard, Ginny said, 'Would you like a drink? A liqueur or something?'

'Are you telling me to mind my own business?'

She smiled. 'Not really.' She poured herself a small glass of Bailey's and went to sit down on the sofa. 'No, it wasn't at all nasty, just rather sad, really. There's a great sense of failure about divorce, even for a marriage as doomed as ours. We were friendly; we still are, in fact. And we carried on as business partners for a while, until...' She was about to say until she became ill, but smoothly changed it to, 'Until Simon decided to come back to England.' There was no point in telling Alex that Simon, in company with many men, had been unable to stand illness in any form and had abandoned her in the clinic. He hadn't done it brutally—there had been lots of flowers and letters from him—but they had both known that was really the end, that he would leave her. And once he was back in England the letters and the flowers had ceased.

'I gather you didn't have any children?'

Ginny looked down at her drink. 'No, it wasn't a begetting kind of marriage. It was just something we drifted into.'

'And is Simon Blake here in England now?'

'Yes, and doing very well again, I understand.'

'Haven't you seen him?'

Ginny shook her head. 'After the telephone was reconnected last week I gave him a call to let him know I was in England, but his secretary said that he was away on an assignment.'

'And he hasn't called you back?'

'I expect he will if he feels like it,' Ginny said casually. 'There's no onus on him to do so.'

Alex gave a sudden frown. 'He's a fool!' he exclaimed forcefully.

Ginny gave him a startled look, then laughed. 'You're right, you *are* possessive.'

He looked momentarily taken aback, but then his eyes glinted with amusement. 'Now you really are telling me to mind my own business.' He gave a bemused shake of his head. 'I can still hardly believe it. But I'm glad you've told me. And there was I feeling so guilty about you when all the time you'd forgotten all about me and married someone else. Just shows you what an egotistical fool I am.' He glanced round. 'Is there any coffee left?'

'Of course.'

Ginny poured him some and he took the cup from her, but, instead of going back to the armchair, sat down beside her on the sofa. For almost the first time since she'd returned to England Alex seemed completely relaxed, the tension gone from his face and shoulders. It was what she'd wanted, what she'd been hoping for, but Ginny hadn't enjoyed telling him about her failed marriage. She had made light of it, of course, but it had been a gruelling, very unhappy time. She had done her best to make it work, but Simon had soon realised that she had given her heart to someone else, and he was shrewd enough to guess who it was. Even though they were fond of each other, he wasn't the kind of man who would accept second-best. They had soldiered on, and there had been some good times, but they had both known it would eventually end.

Venetia's death had been the catalyst, the excuse to finally split up that they had both been expecting and not trying very hard to avoid. Simon had said a couple of things then that had hurt her, perhaps deliberately, and she had been glad to let him go. But she had got over that and the divorce had been amicable, with both of them well enough off not to have any financial squabbles. And now Simon, a born optimist, had embarked on marriage to yet another model, and Ginny was consigned to history as Simon Blake's third wife.

It was a period of her life she didn't enjoy talking about, but telling Alex had been the right thing to do. It had relieved the tenseness between them, so that hopefully they might start again. Leaning back against the sofa, Ginny smiled at Alex. 'Now tell me about your work,' she invited.

It was two o'clock in the morning before Alex left. The music had stopped in the house next door, although the lights were still on. The air felt chilly as Ginny came to the door with him. 'Goodnight.' She stood on the top step and rubbed her hands against her bare arms at the sudden cold.

'Goodnight, Ginny.' Alex hesitated, then leaned forward to briefly kiss her cheek. 'Go in, you're cold.'

But Ginny watched as he walked along the street to where his car was parked, only then, when he'd given her a last wave, going back inside. She ought to have felt tired, but instead she was on a high of almost fearful hope and anticipation. They were no longer enemies, perhaps had even started to become friends, but would they become lovers again? It was almost too wonderful a thought to even dare contemplate. Where Alex was concerned things had gone wrong for her so many times that Ginny was almost afraid to feel optimistic. She was too excited to sleep, too keyed-up to read. Mostly she would have liked to put on a coat and take a long walk, but women alone didn't take walks in a town at two o'clock in the morning, not even in Bath. Ginny washed up cups and glasses, then wandered restlessly around the house. She didn't make any conscious decision, but somehow she found herself outside the door of the unfinished nursery, and slowly reaching out to open it and go inside.

The curtains were drawn back and bright moonlight silvered the teddy-bear wallpaper and the lace-bedecked crib that stood in the corner. The room was very still, with an air of waiting for something that would never come. Ginny didn't turn on the light, but moved further into the room. For a few minutes she thought Venetia's spirit wasn't there any more. Going to the window, she sat on the deep, dusty sill, swinging her legs up in front of her and leaning back against the wall. There was nothing to see through the window except the all-night lights of the retail park. It was very peaceful in here. Ginny's eyelids became heavy and she let them drop, and suddenly her sister's presence was there, all around her.

There was no coldness, only warmth. Ginny's mind drifted back to their childhood when they had been always together, always sharing. Incidents came back into her mind that she had long forgotten, times of happiness when the twins had been at their closest. And times of sadness, too, when their parents had split up and they had been drawn even closer together. But soon warmth and happiness took over again.

Ginny felt as if she was in a beautiful, sunlit place, looking on as she saw herself and Venetia grow from children to young women, still closer than the closest of ordinary sisters. A vivid picture came into her mind of a picnic they had taken together, just the two of them, in the summer before they had met Alex. It had been such a wonderful day, almost the last when they had been alone together. Ginny had thought of it only vaguely since, but now it came back to her in every detail: what they had worn, where they had walked, the flowers they had picked to take home. And as she looked, her eyes almost dazzled by the sunlight, Ginny saw Venetia turn to her and smile—and hold out the flowers in her hand for Ginny to take.

Ginny smiled back and reached out to take them, but felt suddenly very cold and opened her eyes to find herself on the window-seat in the nursery. It was only a dream, she thought, looking round the cold, dusty room; I fell asleep. But her heart was warm with memories and she felt at peace with herself, sure now that Venetia approved of her coming back.

Ginny slept heavily for the rest of that night, not waking until the morning was far gone. She was immediately filled with that 'glad to be alive' feeling that came with youth and the spring. Getting quickly out of bed, Ginny showered and then went for the long walk she'd wanted the night before, striding out through the town in a long raincoat that reached almost to her ankles, her hair loose, but covered by a mannish, brimmed hat to stop the strong wind blowing her hair around. Up near the abbey Ginny came across a stall selling flowers and she bought great armfuls of white lilac and deep red carnations. As she was buying them she heard the abbey bells start to ring out and realised it was already noon. Carrying her flowers, she began to hurry back home.

As she approached the house a car passed her and then pulled into the kerb. It was Alex. He got out as she came nearer and grinned at her. 'Whose birthday is it?'

'Nature's. It's spring.' She smiled back at him, feeling all over again the heart-pulling agony of love.

'Spring?' He said the word on a surprised note, as if he hadn't even noticed what season it was. 'Yes, I suppose it is. You'll fill every vase in the house.'

'They're not all for me. Some are for Clare for last night.'

'The same errand I'm on,' and he indicated a wrapped parcel on the passenger-seat of the car. 'Tell you what; after you've put the flowers in water, why don't we go and have lunch together? There's a pub not too far away that does a good Sunday lunch. Bet you haven't had a decent roast beef and Yorkshire pudding in years.'

Her face lit. 'No, I haven't. I'd love to. If you'll just wait until—— Oh, no! Oh, Alex, I'm sorry, I can't. I've already promised to have lunch with someone I met at the party last night.'

'Of course.' The closed look that Ginny had hoped was gone for good came back into Alex's face.

'Perhaps we could make it some other time?' Ginny said quickly, but he had already bent to get his parcel from the car. 'How about next Sunday?'

'I think Jeff has got something laid on for next weekend.' Alex locked the car and they walked the few yards to her house, but he went on to the

Kennedys'. 'Maybe I'll give you a ring if I'm coming over this way again,' he said offhandedly as he pressed their bell.

The door was opened almost immediately, and he went in without saying goodbye to her. Ginny juggled the flowers to get a hand free to get her key out of her pocket and went inside her own house. She was late. Dropping the flowers in the sink, she ran upstairs to the bedroom to change, but hadn't been there very long when she heard the Kennedys' front door open and close again. Quickly she went to the window and was in time to see Alex walking briskly back to his car. He didn't look round, just got in and drove away. Ginny watched him go, her heart leaden again, muttering, 'Damn. Damn. *Damn!*' in angry frustration.

CHAPTER FIVE

ORDINARILY Ginny would have enjoyed a meal with like-minded girls of her own age, but the thought of Alex walking away, feeling lonely and rejected, kept coming back to spoil things. If only he'd called her earlier, she could have made some excuse to the girls and everything would have been OK. This fragile friendship that they had begun to find last night wouldn't have been slapped down at the first attempt. With an inward sigh, Ginny tried to put him out of her mind and concentrate on being a good guest. Although it was a last-minute invitation, the girls had gone to some trouble, and, after talking about their business for some time, it became clear that they had a proposition to put to Ginny. 'We're looking to expand,' they told her. 'We could use another partner. Someone who could put some capital into the business would be marvellous, of course, but what we're basically looking for is someone with contacts in the right places. Such as yourself.'

'I'm not a businesswoman,' Ginny objected. 'I'm a model. I go wherever there's work. And there's no way I want to be stuck in an office all day.'

'But that isn't what we had in mind. We want a front person, someone as confident as you, who can meet and impress the heads of companies, someone who can even act as a hostess at some of the corporate functions. We just know you would be a terrific asset.'

And maybe she would at that. Thinking about it, Ginny had to agree it was a good idea, from their point of view. But she shook her head. 'I might go back to the States before too long. I really don't know what my plans are.'

'But if you do decide to stay in England, will you think about it?' she was urged.

Ginny nodded. 'All right, but I would only do it on a commission basis. I couldn't be tied down in case it meant losing a good modelling assignment.'

Even this grudging agreement excited them, and Ginny had to admire their enthusiasm. It would have been easy to get caught up in it, too, but she refused to commit herself any further. It was almost five o'clock before she was able to get away and walk home. She had taken some of the flowers as a thank-you for her lunch and now she wrapped some more and took them round to Clare.

'Thanks for the party last night,' she offered as she held out the flowers.

'Oh, that's kind of you. They're beautiful. Come and have a coffee.'

'Oh, but I don't want to intrude.'

'It's OK; Richard is sleeping it off on the settee with the paper over his face, and the kids have gone to my mother's for the weekend and won't be back till this evening.'

They had their coffee in the kitchen, creeping quietly down the stairs so as not to wake Richard, and turning on the lights against the dark storm clouds outside. The room was cosily warmed by the big Aga cooker that Clare used for her baking and kept continually alight, winter and summer. There was a lot of food left over from the party, and Clare picked at it as they talked. She tried to push some cake on to Ginny, but luckily Ginny had her recent lunch as an excuse. 'I wish I was as thin as you,' Clare said enviously as she spread pâté on to a piece of French bread. 'Trouble is I can't stand waste.'

'Which is why you haven't got one,' Ginny said drily.

Clare gave her a startled look and then laughed. 'You're as bad as Venetia was.' She took another bite and said, 'I thought Alex was looking much better.'

'Yes. He enjoyed your party. So did I. You have some nice neighbours.'

But Clare wasn't to be put off. 'You and Alex seemed to be on good terms. Pity you had to leave so early, though.'

'We had some family business to discuss,' Ginny said easily. The overhead lights flickered, came back on, and flickered again before steadying. 'What was that?'

'It's probably the wind,' Clare said with an exasperated frown. 'The wiring in these houses is so old that anything makes the lights go out. The kids had some mice which escaped from their cage—we can't catch them, and sometimes they chew through the electric wires and blow a fuse. Of course Richard is useless with anything like that, so we have to pay the earth to get an electrician in.'

'I bet you have to wait ages, too?' Ginny said sympathetically.

GHOST OF THE PAST

But Clare had a one-track mind, and said in see-through innocence, 'It would be strange if you and Alex got together, wouldn't it? But if he wanted someone to replace Venetia he certainly wouldn't have to look any further. Wouldn't it be romantic? To lose a loved one and then fall in love with her identical twin.'

'Very,' Ginny agreed. 'But hardly likely.' She stood up. 'Thanks for the coffee, but I'm afraid I'll have to go; I have some calls to make.'

'To America?' Clare asked inquisitively.

Ginny did some mental sums and nodded. 'That's right; the coast.'

Suitably impressed, Clare saw her out and waved goodbye. Ginny could imagine her scuttling back to her kitchen and the leftovers, putting her feet up with a magazine; a contented woman for all she'd said she'd like to be slim. Sitting on her own sofa and faced with the telephone, Ginny hesitated. It was true that she had several calls to make, but there was only one person she really wanted to ring. But she wasn't sure whether it would be wise to call Alex so soon. She didn't want to appear to be too eager. Maybe it would be better to play it cool, give him time to phone her first.

In the end this was what she decided to do, but the days passed and Alex didn't call. Her agent, though, did, demanding to know when she was going to go back to work. As the house was more or less finished and Ginny was becoming bored with her own company, she agreed to take on the assignments that her agent had lined up for her, but only those in Europe; she wasn't yet ready to go back to America.

Realising that she was going to be away a lot, Ginny bought an answerphone, listening impatiently to the messages every time she came home, but there was never anything from Alex, although a couple of times someone had rung and replaced the receiver without leaving a message. It wasn't much to go on, but it gave Ginny some hope. After another week, though, when she got home from doing a guest appearance on a panel game and there was still no call from him, Ginny decided that she'd waited long enough. If Alex wouldn't come to her voluntarily, then she would just have to darn well think of something to make him come.

She sat on the sofa, still with her coat on, trying to think. It began to get dark so she reached out to turn on the lamp. It flickered for a moment, reminding her of the conversation she'd had with Clare about the escaped mice. A smile lit her eyes, but then they grew thoughtful. Now where would mice be likely to chew through a wire? In the laundry-room, presumably. It wasn't difficult to find a place near a socket where the plaster was crumbling. Ginny carefully poked at the hole, enlarging it, then turned off all the electricity before jabbing at the wires with a wooden-handled screwdriver; there wouldn't be much point in burning herself to a crisp. When she turned the electricity back on there was a satisfying bang and everything went off again.

Five minutes later she was on the phone to Bristol. 'Alex, I'm sorry to have to bother you, but I've just got home and there seems to be some problem with the electricity supply. Should I try and mend the fuse or something?'

'No. Don't touch anything,' Alex said crisply. 'I'll be right over.'

While she waited, Ginny found some candles and set them out around the sitting-room. They gave the room a mellow, gentle light. This is what it must have been like when the house was built, she thought, and tried to imagine the people who had lived there over the years. She knew little of the history of the house, but guessed that it must have been let to a great many people who were unwell and had come to Bath in the hope that its famous spa waters would cure them. That many hadn't been cured was proved by the hundreds of monuments to the dead that crammed every available wall and pillar space in the abbey, the main church in Bath that she had explored only a week or so earlier.

Ginny sat on the sofa, thinking about Bath and the house, but her mind soon went back to its most recent occupant. Alex had offered to come readily enough, but would he still be distant with her? Would they have lost that first tentative step towards friendship? Theirs was such a strange relationship. Basically she didn't know Alex all that well. They had got on marvellously the first time they had ever met, but then she had seen little of him, and nearly always with Venetia. She had tried, without actually coming out and saying that she loved him, to let him know how she felt, but Alex had misunderstood and thought that she was trying to come between him and Venetia. This had made him angry with her, and so, in despair, Ginny had pretended to be Venetia and spent that one wonderful night with him. So from being enemies they had become as close as any two people could be. But in some ways it would have been better if that hadn't happened, because now it was always there at the back of their minds, the shared passion and the glorious giving and taking of love.

He arrived just as her anticipating heart began to worry that he had changed his mind. 'Hi. Thanks for coming,' she greeted him.

'Can't leave you in the dark,' Alex replied evenly. It was a cool evening and he was wearing a dark-coloured sweater with his jeans.

'I thought of asking Richard next door to help me, but Clare said that he's hopeless at anything practical.'

Alex grinned. 'Yes, he's always found that a convenient excuse.'

That grin was marvellous; it immediately allayed all her fears and brought an answering smile to Ginny's lips. 'Like that, huh?'

'Financial advisers don't mend fuses,' he said, mock serious.

'Just as real mean don't eat quiche?'

'Quite.' He laughed, and it was the best sound in the world. 'But, only being a mere professor and not a financial adviser, perhaps I'd better try and sort out your problem.'

Any time, Ginny thought, but then pulled herself together as she realised that they were still standing in the darkened hall, lit only by the light of the street-lamp outside coming in the fanlight over the door. 'I've got a torch,' she said practically. 'Do you want to look at the fuse-box first?'

'Sounds a good place to start.'

It didn't take Alex long to discover the broken wiring in the laundry-room. Ginny offered Clare's story about the mice, but Alex looked at the hole and said, 'Some mice!'

She didn't know whether he'd guessed that she'd done it herself; she didn't much care. He was here and that was all that mattered. She held the torch for him while Alex did the repair, and in less than half an hour the electricity was back on. 'I'd better come over tomorrow and fill that hole for you,' he remarked, squatting down to look at it in the better light. 'We don't want any more mice getting to the wiring.' He stood up and glanced at her, then looked more closely, seeing her in a good light for the first time. 'You look very glamorous.'

'What?' Ginny realised she was still dressed for the television show in a silver lamé number beneath her jacket. 'Oh, these are my working clothes.'

'What have you been doing?'

She told him over a cup of coffee and he seemed really interested.

'But what about your career in America? Don't you have to go back and work there—keep your name in the public's eye?' he queried.

Ginny's face tightened, but her chin came up as she said, 'You mean I'll be forgotten if I'm not featured in the gossip columns with some celebrity before too long?'

Alex gave her a quizzical look. 'You never did pull your punches. I didn't mean that; I meant your modelling career. Aren't you under contract or something?'

'I'm retained by a couple of fashion houses, but I mostly do freelance work. That's why I was able to come home to England. I thought while I was here

I'd do what work I could; try to be known on both sides of the Atlantic.' She smiled. 'I was even offered a job here in Bath.'

'Really? Doing modelling work?'

'Not quite.' Ginny explained about the two girls with the corporate entertainment business. 'When I went to lunch with them the Sunday after the party they asked me to become a partner; use my contacts to help them expand their business and act as their representative, that kind of thing.'

'The Sunday after Clare's party? Was that who you were having lunch with?'

The surprise in his voice made Ginny say, 'Why, yes. I thought I told you?'

Alex shook his head. 'No, you just said you had a date for lunch.'

And he'd thought it was with a man, of course. No wonder he'd been so abrupt. He must have thought she'd been really fast to fix up a date with some other man at the party and yet have spent most of the evening with him.

'Did you accept their offer?' Alex asked, regaining her attention.

'Not really. I told them that if I was interested at all it would only be on a commission basis, and anyway I don't know how long I'll be over in England.'

'You haven't decided when you're going back to the States, then?'

It was a question Ginny wasn't sure about. Was he eager for her to go—or to stay? Or was he just being politely interested? Carefully keeping her voice light, she said, 'I haven't even given it a thought. It's nice to be back in England after so long; the pace is so much less frenetic. And my London agent seems to be finding me quite a bit of work, here and in Europe.'

Alex put his cup down on the small table beside his chair. 'Have you been mistaken for Venetia yet?'

How to tell him that it was five years since Venetia had dropped out of the London scene and in that time she had long since been forgotten? Ginny didn't try, she just shook her head. 'Not mistaken for her, no.'

'She gave up modelling when we got married.'

'Yes, I know.'

'Was that part of your—bargain?'

'Yes.' She hesitated. 'Didn't Venetia tell you?'

Alex shook his head. 'It—and you—were subjects that we tended to avoid.' He looked round the room, obviously lost in thoughts of the past. 'I wanted to buy Venetia a house in the country, but your father insisted on giving her this one as a wedding present. And she fell in love with it. She'd always liked Bath, of course. She was so much a part of this house.'

'She always will be,' Ginny agreed with certainty, remembering her feeling of closeness to her sister in the nursery.

Alex stood up and for a dreadful moment she thought she'd said the wrong thing again, but he said, 'I'm not dressed for a posh restaurant and you're not dressed for a pub. One of us is going to have to change if we're going to go out and have something to eat.'

Ginny laughed. 'Somehow I have the feeling that it's going to be me.' She held out her hand and let Alex pull her to her feet. For a moment they were close, almost touching—and Alex didn't move away. A tremor ran through her and she quickly took her hand out of his, afraid of letting him see. 'Give me fifteen minutes,' she said lightly, making for the door.

'Oh, yes? Where have I heard that before?'

She did take longer, replacing the heavy television make-up with her own, and changing into designer jeans and a sweater. Grabbing up her bag and jacket, Ginny ran down to join him, and within half an hour, if not a quarter, they were in the car and driving out of town. Ginny felt almost dazed by the success of her ploy; she would willingly have blacked out the whole of Bath for this. And in the same instant she cursed herself for not having made it clear to Alex who she was having lunch with that Sunday. They could have been together like this a whole two weeks earlier and she would have been spared all that mental anguish and uncertainty.

The pub he took her to was in a little village a couple of miles off the main road from Bath to Wells. It was a typical old country pub; they both had to duck their heads as they went through the door, and to avoid the beams in the low ceiling of the bar. Alex had obviously been a regular customer at the pub, because as he went up to the bar to get their drinks the landlord looked up and said, 'Hello, there! Alex Warwick, isn't it? You filled in for us when we were a man short in the cricket eleven one Sunday. That's right; never forget a face. Lucky for the village you were having lunch here that day. Must have been nearly three years ago, wasn't it? Before your wife... We were sorry to hear about that.' His voice had dropped to the low, serious level people always used to talk about the dead, but rose again as he said, 'Glad to see you back here. What can I get you?'

'A pint of beer, please. And a gin and tonic for the lady.'

The landlord looked past him to 'the lady', and froze. 'I'm Alex's sister-in-law,' Ginny said quickly, looking at Alex uneasily. 'Venetia—his wife—was my twin sister.'

'Blimey! You gave me a right turn.'

'You'd better have a drink, then,' Alex said calmly. 'How's the cricket team shaping up for this season?'

They chatted for some minutes and then Alex carried their drinks through to a small restaurant opening off the bar. He didn't say anything about the incident, but Ginny felt that she couldn't just let it go. 'You obviously used to come here a lot with Venetia.'

'Yes, it was one of our favourite places. I haven't been back here since I moved away from Bath, though.'

'Perhaps it would have been better to go somewhere else, somewhere new,' Ginny said awkwardly.

Alex gave her a quick look. 'Has it upset you, coming to a place where I used to take Venetia? I'm sorry.'

'No, I thought it might have upset *you*.'

He shook his head. 'It's a thing you have to get used to, going back to places alone. At first I could hardly bear to go anywhere. I buried myself in my work, stayed in my rooms all my spare time, let the house get neglected. It was Jeff who started pulling me out of it. He made me play squash, tennis, that kind of thing. I even joined him on a couple of holidays, and gradually I began to go back to places that I'd been with Venetia. It just happens that I haven't been here since she died, though. Probably because it's so much nearer to Bath than Bristol.' He gave her a wry grin. 'I'm afraid you're going to have to get used to people mistaking you for Venetia if we're going to go out together in this area.'

Ginny's heart swelled and she felt a great surge of happiness. It was almost too wonderful to dare to contemplate, but for the first time in years it seemed that real, lasting happiness might be in sight. On a far-distant horizon admittedly, but at least it was a possibility. She was here with Alex, they were friends, and the ghost of Venetia was no longer between them. From a beginning like this anything might happen, and definitely would if wishing could make it so. But she would have to tread very carefully, Ginny knew that; she must be careful never to intrude on his past memories, but to convince Alex that there was every possibility of future happiness together.

After their meal at the pub Alex drove her home and dropped her off, refusing an invitation to come into the house. But he came over again the next evening to replaster the 'mouse hole', and did one or two other jobs while he was there. Afterwards they sat in the kitchen drinking coffee and eating a cake that Ginny had bought from Clare.

'Have you redecorated the spare bedroom yet?' Alex asked her.

He never referred to it as the nursery, she noticed. Just as he had never spoken of the unborn child. 'Do you want me to?' she asked carefully.

'Yes.' His reply was definite. 'You were right about my turning this place into some sort of shrine. It was unhealthy. I feel much better about this house now that you and Jeff have changed it. Now I see it for what it is; just a house that I happened to live in for a few years.'

'One in a long line of owners and tenants.'

'Yes.' He nodded, looking pleased that she understood.

'I was thinking about that yesterday, when the candles were lit; wondering about all the people who must have lived here in the past. So much must have happened here. People being born, falling in love, living out their lives.'

'More likely being let out to people taking the waters at the highest possible rents the owners could get,' Alex said prosaically.

Ginny pulled a face at him. 'How unromantic you are.'

'So Venetia always used to say.' He gave her a direct look. 'Will you redo that bedroom?'

She nodded. 'Yes, all right. What shall I do with—with the things in it?'

'Get rid of them,' he said firmly. 'Give them to someone who can use them, or a charity shop or something.'

'And Venetia's clothes?'

'Are they still here?' he asked in surprise. And when she nodded again, 'Give those away, too.' Alex hesitated. 'I'd rather you didn't keep them and wear them yourself.'

'No, I won't do that. And I'll start on the room this weekend.'

'Let me know when it's—clear, and I'll come and give you a hand.'

'What about Jeff? He'll think you're doing him out of a job.'

Alex grinned. 'Jeff has other things on his mind at the moment. An old student of his has moved into this area and looked him up. He's busy showing her the sights of Bristol.'

'Really?' Ginny was immediately intrigued. 'What's she like? Does he really like her?'

With a burst of laughter, Alex said, 'You're trying to marry him off. You're as bad as Venetia was.' He stopped, his face changing. 'I'm sorry, I shouldn't keep saying that.'

'Why not? Venetia and I were very much alike, not only to look at.' Ginny smiled. 'And, unlike you, *we* were both very romantic.'

Alex lifted his hands in surrender. 'OK. OK. I don't know much about Jeff's new girl except that her name is Kay, short for Katherine, that she's got a job in Bristol, and she has a history degree.'

'She's clever, then?'

There was a defensive note in her voice that Alex recognised and which brought a look of surprise to his eyes. 'You too? Venetia always had a slight inferiority complex where university graduates were concerned. I always used to tell her that she was as good as they were any day.'

Ginny looked amused. 'I quite agree with you. But I think you'll find that in my case the apprehension is because most graduates, when they find out you didn't go to college, always flaunt their *superiority* complexes.'

Alex gave her a startled look and then laughed in admiration. 'Well done! You're far more confident than—you're extremely confident. I suppose it comes from those years in America. And from being so successful.'

'I don't have to prove anything to anyone, if that's what you mean.'

His grey eyes grew thoughtful. 'No, I don't suppose you do. I've never been—close to a celebrity before. It's difficult to think of you as that, of you hob-nobbing with the rich and famous. But I suppose that you're rich and famous, too?'

'I don't consider myself to be. Just lucky enough to be successful in my chosen career, that's all.'

'I'm sure you're being over-modest. You must have worked very hard to get where you are.'

'Yes,' Ginny acknowledged. 'It has been hard work.'

'But suitably well paid. I suppose you could retire tomorrow, if you wanted to?'

A tricky question to answer, because she didn't know which way he wanted her to answer it. So Ginny just smiled and said, 'Twenty-six is rather young to think about retiring,' and quickly changed the subject.

The next day Ginny cleared the baby things out of the nursery and took them to a charity shop in Cheltenham; far enough away for there to be abso-lutely no chance of Alex ever seeing them again. That afternoon she spent at her mother's house, but Ginny returned to Bath the same evening and spent the next day scraping off the teddy-bear wallpaper, so that when Alex came round to help her that weekend there was nothing to remind him that it had ever been in-tended as a nursery. He noticed its absence, of course, but said nothing, just got on with the job of painting the ceiling.

Ginny had chosen wallpaper for this room, so it took longer to do, and during that weekend and the following evenings when they worked together their friendship grew and gradually became more relaxed. Ginny sensed that Alex was grateful for her sensitivity in scraping off the wallpaper, but knew that the original use he'd meant for the room must always be there in the back of his mind. So she made him talk a lot while they worked, finding out about the years when they had been apart, and in return telling him about herself. But they talked generally, only referring in passing to Venetia and Simon Blake, and then only as people who had been part of the past.

'I'll have to have a curtain made and buy new furniture for this room,' Ginny remarked enthusiastically on the evening when it was finished. She was standing in the middle of the room, hands on hips, looking round, obviously pleased with the result.

'Can't you make the curtain yourself?'

Ginny, sensitive to all his moods, recognised the slight pause before he had spoken and guessed that he had been going to say that Venetia used to make all her own curtains, but had changed it in time. It was a good sign, she thought. It showed he was thinking of her.

'I don't think I'd make a very good job of it,' she admitted frankly. 'I was never that good at sewing. And anyway I won't have time; if you remember, I have that modelling assignment in London next week.'

'Will you be staying up in town the whole week?'

'Yes, it hardly seems worth driving back every night.'

Alex finished wiping down the woodwork and stood back. 'There. How does that look?'

'It looks great. You've done a marvellous job.'

He shook his head. 'We both have.' He turned to smile at her. 'And I think we both deserve a drink.'

It was a fine evening, so they sat outside in the garden, Alex drinking a beer and Ginny a long drink. She had done quite a bit of work on the garden in the two weeks when she had waited in vain for Alex to call, but it had become so overrun that there was still a lot to do. Their drinks in their hands, they walked round the garden, Alex pointing out the different plants, telling Ginny when they were planted, and where he and Venetia had bought them. 'That rose we bought to commemorate our first anniversary,' he told her, indicating a climbing yellow rose that almost smothered the wall. Inevitably it brought a feeling of sadness to them both, but Ginny was pleased that he felt able to talk about Venetia with her, was no longer bottling things up inside.

'It needs pruning,' she remarked.

'So it does.'

She hadn't meant him to think of it as a job, but Alex went into the laundry-room, came back with a step-ladder and a pair of rather rusty secateurs, and began to cut back the suckers. Getting her gardening gloves, Ginny began to clear up after him and they worked well together until a particularly vicious thorn went through her glove into her thumb. 'Ouch!'

'Pricked yourself?'

'Mm.' Ginny carefully peeled off her glove. 'Darn. It's gone right in.'

'Here, better let me take a look.' Alex climbed down from the ladder and examined her thumb. 'It's going to take a pair of tweezers to get it out.'

'I've got a pair in the bathroom; I'll get them.'

The evening was drawing in, so they went into the kitchen where the light was better while Alex cleaned her thumb with antiseptic before probing with the tweezers. Ginny flinched a little and gave a gasp as he firmly pulled out the thorn. He laughed and put a comforting arm round her. 'Come on, that didn't hurt. You always were a little coward.' He kissed her on the nose in easy intimacy. 'Why, I remember when you——' He saw the sudden surge of happiness in her eyes and broke off abruptly. The hand that held hers began to shake uncontrollably.

Quickly Ginny put hers over it and held his hand tightly. 'It's all right, Alex.'

But his face had gone ashen. 'For a moment there I forgot who you were. I thought you were——'

'It was bound to happen,' she said swiftly, not wanting him to finish.

'Was it?' He pulled his hand free and doubled it into a tightly controlled fist, his jaw tightening. Turning away, he replaced the top on the antiseptic bottle before facing her again. His face bleak, Alex said curtly, 'I'm not sure this is such a good idea, Ginny. Seeing you, being with you, especially in this house; it brings Venetia back into my mind all the time.'

Sudden fear gripped her heart, but Ginny managed to say, 'That's inevitable, I suppose.'

'But it isn't fair on either of us,' Alex burst out. 'Especially on you. You deserve better than to be mistaken for someone else, even for a moment.' He ran a hand through his hair. 'I don't want to think of you as just taking Venetia's place.'

'I don't want that either.'

He gave her a brooding look. 'But maybe that's inevitable, too. Maybe we're making a big mistake in hoping that we can even be friends.'

Ginny bit her lip, trying hard to be calm. 'Aren't you any happier than you were?'

He nodded rather reluctantly, but said honestly, 'Yes, I must admit I am. But in some ways even that seems to be wrong. It's as if I'm betraying Venetia's memory.'

'That's stupid,' Ginny said at once, so forcefully that his head jerked up to look at her. 'Do you really think that Venetia would have wanted you to go on being sad for the rest of your life? Go on grieving for her, yes, by all means. But that doesn't mean that you can't look for happiness again, surely?'

His mouth twisted ruefully. 'Do you think I don't know that? But it's easy to tell yourself so; quite another to get into the mental state where you can put it into practice.' Alex shook his head. 'I don't know, Ginny. I *am* happier now than I've been since she died. But is it because I'm starting to get over it and I'm enjoying your company—or is it because subconsciously I'm putting you in Venetia's place, pretending that you're her? That she's still alive?'

'Oh, God, please don't do that, Alex,' Ginny pleaded urgently.

'Do you think I want to?' He caught her arm in sudden violence, and then gripped it hard as he added, 'But maybe I do. Maybe that is what I want. To go on as if nothing had happened. To shut out all the years of hurt and pain. To go back to the life we had.' His eyes, bleak and tortured, raked her face. 'What if that's what I want, Ginny? Could you do that, for me?'

It would have been so easy to say yes, yes, I love you and I'll do anything you want. But that way led only to madness and self-destruction. Pulling away from him, Ginny gripped the back of the chair, putting it between them. 'No. You can't ever go back,' she said fiercely, 'It's impossible. Trying to would only make us hate each other. You must see that.'

'Yes, of course.' He gritted his teeth for a moment, his eyes closed. 'You're quite right, of course. I'm sorry.' He turned away, went to the sink to wash his hands.

Going to him, Ginny put her hand on his shoulder and felt his body tense. Her heart breaking for him, she said persuasively, 'Anyone in your position, any widow or widower, must go through the same emotional trauma, the same feelings of betrayal when they meet someone else. You're not unique, Alex.'

He gave a short laugh as he turned to pick up the towel. 'I may not be, but our situation probably is. Look at it from your own point of view, Ginny. Everyone who sees us together must think that I'm using you to replace Venetia. Do you really want that?'

'It wouldn't worry me as long as I was sure that you knew you weren't.'

He gave an angry shrug. 'But that's just it, isn't it? I don't know. We're back where we started. Maybe it would help if we kept away from each other for a while, saw other people.'

Ginny thought with sinking heart of the two weeks when she had waited for him to phone. 'I don't think it will make any difference. It certainly won't to me. I don't see why we can't be friends.'

'Friends?' He gave her a brooding look. 'I'm beginning to think that just friendship isn't possible. We both know it, don't we? After—what happened between us in the past, I think any relationship we have now would have to be all or nothing.'

'Perhaps,' she acknowledged, her heart racing. 'But that doesn't mean that we can't take our time over finding out, does it? Personally I'm in no great hurry to get into a permanent relationship again. I certainly don't intend to drift into one. I want to be sure of myself next time, if there ever is a next time,' Ginny added, her hands gripping the chair.

'There has to be a next time for you,' Alex said firmly. 'You're too young and beautiful to be alone. You're made for love, Ginny. And you deserve to be happy.' He sighed. 'And maybe I'm being extremely selfish in wanting to keep you here while I try and work things out when you ought to be meeting a man who could love you without reservation.'

A gleam of amusement came into Ginny's eyes. 'Egotistical rather than selfish, perhaps. If I get to know you better I might not want to stay around.'

Alex gave her a sudden grin, the grin that she remembered from the old days. 'Ouch! That took me down a few dozen pegs. Maybe you're right at that.'

He gave her a thoughtful look. 'You're going to be away all next week; maybe for both our sakes you should use the time to really think about us, decide what you want, if you think we have any chance of a future.'

'Surely even the smallest chance is worth pursuing?' Ginny objected.

'Maybe. But I want you to think selfishly, Ginny. I've changed, and so have you. Perhaps it would be better if we walked away from this.'

'And you? Are you going to think about it, too?'

'I doubt if I'll be able to think of much else,' he said wryly. 'I'll probably find myself writing your name on the lecture-room board.'

'As long as it's my name you write and not Venetia's,' Ginny couldn't help saying, out of disappointment and despair.

His eyes shadowed. 'Which brings us round full circle again.' Alex turned to go. 'Goodbye, Ginny. Enjoy your trip to London.'

'Alex.' She ran after him as he went up the stairs and caught him in the hall. 'You'll let me know? Either way, you must promise to let me know.'

'Of course. And you.' But they both knew that it would be his decision. 'When are you due back?'

'A week on Friday. In the evening. About nine, I expect.'

'OK. I'll either be here—or I'll leave you a letter. Bye, Ginny.' And he let himself out.

By the end of the following week Ginny felt both mentally and physically drained. She just couldn't go through another week like that, wondering what Alex was thinking, whether he had come to a decision. She wanted to call him but didn't dare, afraid of influencing him against her. She did her work and did it well, glad to escape into it. She saw her London agent and went out to lunch with a producer who'd seen her in the television panel game and was interested in offering her a part in a charity spectacular he was staging. Careerwise everything was going well, and she seemed to be making an impact on England. Ginny also took the time to look up old friends and, after hesitating a while, called her ex-husband again. Simon was at home this time and they had a drink together later. It was nice to see him, nice to think that they could be friends. Ginny even felt some of the old affection for him, but could see now that that was all it had ever been. They parted on good terms and Ginny was left to long for the end of the week.

It came at last, and she took the train to Bath. To make her life perfect, Alex would have been waiting at the station for her, but he wasn't there. Well, OK, she hadn't specifically told him which train she would be on. The train had been late and the taxi she took from the station seemed to crawl along the streets, but it arrived at the house at last. It was still daylight, so she couldn't tell by looking at the windows whether Alex was there. The taxi-driver carried her cases up the steps and into the hall for her, then was surprised to find the fare and a large tip shoved into his hand and the door closed behind him.

'Alex! Alex, I'm back.' Ginny ran into the sitting-room and then flew down to the kitchen. But the house was just as she'd left it, completely undisturbed. Ginny looked at her watch and checked it

against the kitchen clock. A quarter past nine. Slowly
she went back up the stairs. On the hall table there
were several letters that Clare must have put there
when she came in to water the plants, but on the
doormat, unnoticed as she had rushed in, there was
a solitary envelope without a stamp. Slowly, reluctantly, Ginny went to pick it up.

CHAPTER SIX

GINNY picked up the envelope, her hand trembling and her eyes filling with tears so that she couldn't see the writing properly. She went to open it, but as she fumbled with the flap heard the sound of a key being turned in the lock. She stood, frozen, as the front door opened and Alex walked in.

He stopped in surprise at seeing her so near, then came in and closed the door. 'Hello, Ginny.' His gaze went to her pale, still face and his eyes shadowed. He seemed to make an effort, and after a moment said, 'I came to tell you that I've thought things over and I'd very much like to go on from where we were. But it looks as if you've had second thoughts. That's quite understandable, of course.' The closed look came into his face and he straightened his shoulders. 'You're very wise. I'll go and——'

The shock wave receded at last, bringing back life to her senses, and Ginny said sharply, 'Alex. Just shut up, will you?' And stepped into his arms.

For a moment he just held her, taken aback by the sudden change. But then Alex looked down at Ginny and said, 'Are you sure?'

'Yes.' Her reply was definite. 'I've never been in any doubt.'

'Well, that's nice to know. For a moment there——'

But Ginny shook him impatiently. 'Aren't you going to kiss me, you big oaf?'

Alex laughed delightedly, but then his eyes softened and he bent to touch his mouth against hers. At first it wasn't a kiss, just an exploration of an action that he vaguely remembered. His lips were cool, undemanding, even hesitant. But Ginny wasn't having that. After a few minutes she put her arms around his neck and held her body close against his as she kissed him properly, the kind of kiss that demanded a response from any red-blooded male. And she got it. Alex gave a strange kind of groan and then his arms tightened around her, his shoulders hunching as he returned the kiss in swift and searing passion, his body trembling. Ginny yielded to it happily, greedily, but, even as she began to drown in his embrace, at the back of her mind she prayed: let him be thinking of me. Please let him be thinking of me and not Venetia.

It was the first real kiss Alex had ever given her knowing that it was her, Ginny, and not her sister. And for Ginny it didn't last anywhere near long enough. It seemed only a moment before Alex was straightening up, holding her away from him. His body was shaking and there was sweat on his lip. He saw the disappointment in her eyes and put up a hand to draw it over his face. 'Sorry. I got rather more than I bargained for there.' He gave her a direct look, wanting her to understand. 'It's been—it's been a hell of a long time.'

She did understand. It had been a hell of a long wait for her, too; five whole years of waiting and longing for something she had never really expected to find again. There had been Simon in the meantime, of course, but it had never been the same; sex with Simon had been pleasant because he had had plenty of experience and knew how to please a woman, but there had been no overwhelming desire, no feeling of glory in the giving, no warmth and love to raise the act above the mundane. But for Alex it had been different. He had found his love, his happiness; there hadn't been any years of frustrated longing. And she was sure that since Venetia had died he had been celibate. It would feel strange for him to be sexually aroused, sexually close to another woman. Even though they had shared that one night long ago. So she must play it cool, Ginny realised. Let him get used to the idea and make all the running. Well, OK, she had waited this long, she could wait a little longer. And maybe taking it slow would make their relationship that much closer, would add to the magic when they finally made love again.

So Ginny smiled at him and said, 'Serves you right for being late; I thought you weren't coming. I thought this letter was from you.' And she showed him the envelope that was still clutched in her hand. 'It was on the mat.'

'Have you only just arrived?'

'Yes, I got held up in the traffic.'

'So did I. Must be a traffic hold-up in the town somewhere.' He smiled at her. 'Have you eaten yet?'

'No, not since lunch.'

'What would you like to do, then? We could go out for a meal or I could go and get a Chinese take-away, if you'd prefer it.'

Remembering her decision to play it cool, Ginny said, 'Let's go out. The house doesn't seem very welcoming at the moment.'

He nodded, and she thought he was pleased, perhaps even relieved. Whatever Alex wanted from her, it wasn't an immediate mad, passionate affair. Picking up the rest of her post, she followed him out to his car. It was too late to drive out to the country pub, so they settled for a restaurant in the town that did traditional English food, things like steak and kidney pudding, and spotted dick, mostly catering for the foreign tourist market.

'Who was your letter from?' Alex asked her, after they'd given their order.

Ginny took the letter from her bag, not afraid now to open the envelope. 'It's from the two girls with the entertainment business,' she said after scanning it. 'They want to know if I'd act as hostess for a sports clothing firm that have booked them to organise a party during Wimbledon week.'

'And will you?'

'If they offer me enough money and I'm not already booked for another job.'

Alex grinned at her. 'I like your attitude.'

Ginny sorted through the rest of her post. 'These all seem to be bills.' She tossed them back in her bag. 'Were you busy while I was away?'

'No.' Alex looked into her eyes. 'I missed you.'

Ginny's heart gave a crazy jump and her eyes lit, but she merely said lightly, 'That's nice.'

'And I mean *you*. It wasn't the same—ache of loneliness that I've felt since Venetia died. I missed your wit and sparkle, and the enthusiasm that you bring to everything.'

'That's even nicer,' Ginny said unsteadily. 'Thanks. I'm glad.' She reached across the table and Alex took her hand in his, without any hesitation. That felt good, too.

'So tell me about all the glamorous things you've been doing while you were in London.'

'Not that glamorous; hard work mostly. There was the fashion show, which was the most important. That took four days, what with the rehearsal and a charity show. Then I did a day's photographic modelling for a magazine, and also appeared in a television show, although that probably won't be shown for some time. Apart from that I looked up some old friends and had dinner with——' she hesitated and picked up her drink '—with another old friend.'

Alex gave her a keen look. 'With Simon Blake?'

She nodded reluctantly. 'Yes.'

'Who did the looking up, you or he?'

'I did, as a matter of fact. I'm still—fond of him. I wanted to be sure that he's OK.'

'And is he?'

Ginny gave a small laugh and shrugged. 'As well as he'll ever be now, I suppose. He's married again, to another model, and he's happy enough for the moment. But I don't think it will last. Simon misses his kids and a family life too much. He should never have parted from his first wife really, but he had an affair with a model and his wife found out. And instead of riding it out she gave him an ultimatum: her and the kids or get out. Like a fool, he let his pride get in the way and he left. But I think that in his heart he's regretted it ever since, although he has far too much male pig-headedness to admit it, of course.'

'It's a shame you didn't realise all that before you married him.'

'Yes, I suppose so.'

Alex gave her a sharp look. 'Don't you regret marrying him?'

'Not in the circumstances, no.'

'The circumstances?'

But she just shook her head, not prepared to tell him that she had married Simon out of feelings of total despair because Alex was lost to her, and a need to convince herself that she still had a life to lead and a right to find happiness where she could. That she hadn't been able to find it had been the second tragedy in her young life, and had given her a feeling of guilt where Simon was concerned, although he had never accused her of marrying him for the wrong reasons until the very end, when they had both known for some time that it was over—and she would be eternally grateful to him for that.

Alex gave her a thoughtful look, but let her change the subject when she asked about Jeff and his new girlfriend.

'Yes, he's still going out with Kay. How would you feel about our all going out together some time? A colleague of ours has a boat at Bristol and he often lends it to Jeff and me. We thought maybe we could all go sailing one weekend.'

'That sounds great,' Ginny said eagerly. 'I'd love to. When?'

'Probably next weekend, if Kay is free.'

'I'll have to get myself some suitable clothes.'

Alex laughed. 'You're as bad as Venetia. She always had to have the clothes to fit the occasion.'

'So what's wrong with that?' Ginny retorted. Their meal came and she began to eat, thinking that the sailing boat trip would not only be fun, but it would be a relief to be with someone new, someone who had never known Venetia and who wouldn't wonder at her and Alex being together.

After their meal Alex dropped her off at the house, but wouldn't come in, saying that he knew she had to unpack. 'I'll call you tomorrow to let you know if it's OK for the weekend,' he told her. He took her hand, hesitated briefly, but then drew her to him and kissed her. It wasn't a very satisfactory kiss in the confines of the car, and afterwards Alex smiled ruefully. 'I can do better than that.'

'I know,' she reminded him softly.

'So you do.' He put his hand up to gently stroke the back of his hand across her cheek. 'Take care, Ginny.'

'And you.' She got out of the car and waved as he drove away, then let herself into the house in spirits so elated that she felt she was floating on a euphoric cloud of happiness.

The boat trip was definitely fixed for next weekend, Alex told her when he rang the next morning. 'We'll leave on the Saturday morning and come back Sunday evening. That OK with you?'

'Why, yes. Fine.' But Ginny was taken aback to find that they would be out on the boat overnight; she had expected it to be just a day-trip.

It was a beautifully warm day. Ginny sorted out her washing and put it in the machine, then took her cup of coffee out into the garden. It looked different. The tiny lawn had been cut and several of the plants that climbed up the high surrounding wall had been pruned and tied back. Alex must have been here while she was away. The borders were full of flowers and the roses had started to come out, making bright splashes of yellow against the old brick wall. Feeling more content than she had done for years, Ginny sat in one of the garden chairs, leaning her head back to feel the sun on her face, enjoying the peace of the garden and the scent of the yellow roses. The yellow roses that were Venetia's favourite flower. The thought brought a flicker of icy coldness into her heart. How often must her sister have sat here in the garden, looking forward to a long life of similar content? But poor Venetia's life had been so short. Fighting off a terrible feeling of dread and premonition, Ginny quickly drank her coffee, then went round to Clare's to take the sweater she had bought for her neighbour as a thank-you for looking after the house.

Ginny saw Alex twice more that week, once when they played tennis together, and the second time when they went to see a film. On both occasions he kissed her when they met and when they said goodnight; the kisses were warm and tender, but Ginny sensed that he wasn't yet ready to demonstrate any deeper feelings. Perhaps he still had to get used to the idea that he could feel passion again; his reaction to that kiss when he'd told her he wanted to go on seeing her had certainly shaken him.

Ginny bought some clothes for the weekend in a good shop in Cheltenham when she went over to visit her mother: practical new jeans and shorts, a striped

T-shirt and a fun sweatshirt with 'Anchors Aweigh!' written on the back. She also bought a very cut-away swimsuit that did everything to enhance her figure, a figure that was a little more rounded than it had been when she left America. Not that that was at all a bad thing, careerwise, because models with curves were actually coming back into fashion.

They were setting off early on Saturday morning, because of the tide, Alex had informed her, so Ginny drove over to Bristol to meet the others. She found the men at the marina, busily loading up the boat with enough supplies to last them for a week by the look of it. Ginny smiled as she collected her tote-bag and walked towards them, thinking how happy and boyish they looked.

'Hi.' Alex saw her and came to take her bag from her. He kissed her on the mouth, to anyone else a casual kiss but to them an important step forward for him to do so in front of Jeff.

'Hi.' She gave him a smile that was just for him, then went to greet Jeff, kissing him, too. 'So where is she? I'm longing to meet Kay.'

'She should be here any minute. We told her seven o'clock.'

'And a most ungodly hour it is,' Ginny informed them, but she had enjoyed her ride through the early morning countryside, the villages still asleep. 'Can I help?'

'You can start stowing the food away in the galley, if you wouldn't mind.'

Alex had already described the boat to her so she knew it was a thirty-foot sailing yacht, called *Lydian*, but she hadn't expected it to be so new or so graceful.

The galley was in the middle of the boat and had all the latest gadgets: a fridge, a microwave oven, a washer-dryer. They certainly wouldn't be roughing it as she'd half expected. She began to sort out the food, but after only a few minutes Alex called down to her, 'Kay's coming.'

Climbing over a case of beer cans, Ginny went up on deck and down the gangplank on to the quay. Kay was about her own age, but with a mop of unruly dark curls, a diffident smile, and only about five feet four in height. When she walked up to join them, they all three towered over her. Kay looked round at them and said, 'Oh, *dear*,' in such a heartfelt way that they all burst into laughter.

It made for a good start, especially when Ginny said, 'Believe me, Kay, you're at a great advantage, because you're the only one of us who is going to be able to stand up inside that boat.'

They left as soon as everything was on board, using the engine as they left the marina and made their way down the river through the steep sided Avon Gorge and under the Clifton suspension bridge, famous for its number of suicides. Then they were out into the mouth of the River Severn and turning towards the sea. Ginny was sitting up in the prow with Alex, enjoying the sun, but now a thought occurred to her. 'I suppose you and Jeff do know how to handle this boat?'

'What a time to ask!' He ruffled her already windswept hair and put his arm round her waist, holding her close against him.

It was a great start to a great day. Ginny quickly found her sea-legs and loved every minute of it, although Kay wasn't quite so happy and disappeared below a couple of times when they got to the open sea. Ginny went to see that she was all right and took the opportunity to suss out the sleeping arrangements. The boat could sleep eight, evidently; there were three double cabins—but only one of them with a double bed—and two extra bunks in the cockpit. The men's bags had been tossed into one of the cabins, but as no one had yet unpacked that didn't mean a thing.

Hugging the coast, they sailed along the Somerset and north Devon coastline, the sails picking up the breeze and carrying them along at a fair rate. Ginny prepared sandwiches for their lunch and Kay came down into the galley to help, but just sat there, looking green.

'Do they often go sailing?' she asked rather desperately.

Sensing that an affirmative reply might mean the end of Jeff's romance, Ginny said firmly, 'Hardly at all, I should think. If they were really keen on it they would probably have bought a boat of their own instead of borrowing this one, don't you think? Here, try this—for medicinal purposes.' And Ginny gave her a tot of brandy.

It brought some natural colour back to Kay's pale cheeks. 'You've known Jeff for quite a long time, haven't you?'

'Yes, but I didn't see him for about five years, when I was in America.'

'But you used to go out together?'

Busy making sandwiches, Ginny hadn't realised where the questions were leading, but now it occurred to her that Kay was in a similar position to that *she* had once been in with Alex and Venetia. 'We made up a four a few times,' she answered, making it sound very casual.

'He seems to be—very fond of you.'

'He was very kind to me when I was pretty low one time.'

'But you prefer Alex?'

Ginny turned to Kay and smiled. 'Yes, I prefer Alex.'

That smile gave Kay all the reassurance she wanted. She managed a small smile back, but, her mental anxieties appeased, she was able to think of her surroundings again and said, 'I do wish I didn't feel so ill.'

'Perhaps there are some anti-seasickness pills in the first-aid locker; why don't you have a look?'

Kay found some and was able to join them while they were having lunch, anchored in a bay off Lynton, the sun beating down on the deck where they sat, though she couldn't bring herself to have anything to eat. The poor girl did her best not to show it, but it was obvious that she wasn't enjoying herself.

'Maybe we should go back,' Ginny suggested.

'No, no. I shall be fine as soon as I get used to it,' Kay protested. 'These pills are helping a lot.'

Realising that she didn't want to spoil it for them, they went on in the afternoon. Kay went down below again and Ginny found her having another swig from the brandy bottle. 'Are you sure you're all right? We can very easily turn back and go home.'

But Kay said, 'No, I'm fine. Really.'

The men had intended to anchor for the night and cook a meal on board, but when Ginny went on deck again she beckoned them to her and said, 'Kay's really feeling rough, but she won't give in. Do you think we could go into a harbour this evening and have a meal on land?'

The relief on Kay's face when they tied up at Bideford and she stood on dry land again was worth losing several hours of sailing. They strolled through the town for a while before finding a little restaurant near the harbour that specialised in seafood caught fresh that day. It wasn't an over-smart place, just with check tablecloths on old wooden tables, benches for seats, and stuffed fish in cases round the walls. The patrons seemed to be all sailors of one kind or another, both professional and weekend, giving the place an immediate atmosphere of warmth and friendliness. Ginny could imagine the thousands of sailing stories that had been told over the beer and house wine.

The restaurant was full and the service slow, but no one seemed to mind. The air was rich with noise and laughter and the smell of cooking. The four of them squeezed on to a table set closely between two others and soon found themselves chatting to their neighbours on either side. They drank a carafe of wine while waiting for their food and another one with it, their talk extending along the tables as if it was one big party. At ten a man with an accordion came in and started to sing sea-shanties, everyone joining in to roar out the choruses, banging their beer mugs on the tables.

They didn't leave until the restaurant closed at nearly midnight, calling goodnight to people with whom they had been on the friendliest terms for a few hours and whom they would never see again; a little oasis of human naturalness and conviviality in an over-civilised world. Alex put his arm round Ginny's waist, holding her close against his side. 'It's a nice night; why don't we take a walk before we turn in?' he suggested. He called out to Jeff, saying they'd see them later, and turned away from the town to walk along by the water.

It was a beautiful night, almost tropically warm, the stars bright in the still sky. A night for lovers, Ginny thought, and her heart ached with longing. Would the time be right tonight? she wondered, hardly daring to hope. Would Alex take her down into the dark little cabin, and would he undress her and make love to her again, taking her back to the wonder and magic of that other night so long ago? He was certainly relaxed tonight; there was no tension in the body close against hers. They came to an open stretch of land with a view across the estuary. The moon was out, silvering the water, so beautiful that it hurt the eyes and brought a lump of sentiment to their throats.

'It ought always to be like this,' Ginny said dreamily.

'Mm.' Alex leaned against a tree-trunk and pulled her to him. He found her mouth in small, exploring kisses that both teased and delighted. Ginny tilted her head back, letting him trace the long column of her neck with his lips, his breath hot against her skin. She gave a low moan and moved her hips against his, her being filled with the exquisite sensation of desire and need. He found her mouth again and his kiss deepened, became demanding, his hands low on her waist, holding her against him. Ginny lifted her arms to put her hands on either side of his head, avidly returning his embrace, greedily savouring the kisses she had hungered for.

'Ginny. Ginny.' Alex breathed the name on a long sigh, almost as if he were saying it for the first time.

His hand went to her breast, exploring gently but exciting her almost beyond control. She wanted to cry out to him to make love to her now. Now! She wanted him to bear her down on the grass and tear her clothes off, to show her the overwhelming, uncontrolled passion that she knew he was capable of. A great tremor ran through her and she clung to him, hardly able to breathe.

'Ginny?'

She took a deep, shuddering breath, belatedly remembering that she must let him make all the moves. She mustn't be too eager, too hungry. Using all her strength of mind, she managed a small laugh. 'I'm so hot!'

'You can say that again,' Alex agreed with a grin.

Ginny smiled, but said, 'Maybe we should go back to the boat?'

'OK.' But he kissed her again, very efficiently, before they turned and strolled back, their arms round each other's waist.

I must forget that we once made love, Ginny told herself as they walked along. This must be a courtship for us. An old-fashioned word to describe a growing relationship that must be gradual and unhurried. She knew they must get to know each other in the accepted sense so that they would have every chance of finding something lasting. In her case mind must rule desire. And in Alex's? Perhaps mind would have to be subjugated before desire could surface. But at least tonight had shown that he had made a very good start, she thought with a chuckle.

Alex's arm tightened. 'What's so amusing?'

She put both arms round his waist and smiled up at him, the moon giving an added radiance to her face. 'I'm just happy,' she said simply. 'Aren't you?'

The question took him by surprise, and his answer even more. 'Yes,' he said. 'I think I am.'

But then his eyes shadowed and she knew he was thinking of Venetia, so Ginny quickly laughed and said, 'Those sea-shanties; where did you learn them? You and Jeff knew all the words, including the unauthorised versions, I might add.'

'Well, we've been sailing once or twice before.'

They talked safely about past sailing trips until they reached the boat. There were lights on in the galley and the aft cabin.

'Looks as if Kay may have gone to bed,' Alex remarked.

They crept quietly on board, the boat swaying under their weight, and found Jeff sitting in the galley, a mug of cocoa in front of him.

'How's Kay?'

'A bit wobbly,' he admitted with a rueful grin. 'I think the wine must have gone to her head. She's gone to bed.' Not only the wine but the 'medicinal' brandy, too, Ginny thought, but didn't say anything. 'I think it might be a good idea if I looked in on her now and again. I've an idea she isn't going to sleep very much tonight.'

'I'll stay with her,' Ginny offered.

But Jeff shook his head decidedly. 'No, she's my responsibility. I'll take care of her.' He glanced at Alex. 'Although I'm afraid your sleep will be disturbed if we share a cabin.'

Alex shrugged, but then glanced at Ginny before saying slowly, 'Maybe I'll share Ginny's, then, if she doesn't mind.'

She shook her head, too overwhelmed to speak.

'I'll turn in, then.' Jeff stood up and promptly banged his head on the ceiling. Uncharacteristically, he swore, making Ginny and Alex burst into smothered laughter. Jeff grinned. 'Wait till you do it.'

Ginny used the tiny bathroom and went into the cabin to undress. Expecting to have to share a cabin with Kay, she had brought a pair of shorty pyjamas with her in cool cotton with convict's arrows and 'Jailbird' written across the front. She was brushing her hair as Alex knocked. 'Ginny? You decent?'

'Yes. Come in,' she called, her heart thumping.

He burst into laughter when he saw her pyjamas, bringing things back to normal. 'I expected you to be wearing something sophisticated and silky,' he told her.

Ginny wrinkled her nose at him. 'I like fun clothes.'

He grinned at her. 'You're just a big kid.'

The cabin had a double bed but their sleeping-bags were single ones. Ginny wriggled into her bag and Alex leaned over her to open the window on her side of the cabin, the water side. He was wearing just a T-shirt and shorts, but he pulled off the shirt when he got into his sleeping-bag. Ginny tried not to look at his body, tried not to remember the heights of pleasure it had once carried her to. He clicked off the light and lay back.

'Goodnight,' Ginny said into the darkness.

Alex reached for her hand and carried it to his lips. 'Goodnight, Ginny. My sweet Ginny.'

Her heart swelled in deep content. No matter that he had often to repeat her name to remind himself who she was, tonight they were close and she was immeasurably happy. She would hold on to this moment, she thought, lie here with Alex's hand in hers and make it last. But she fell asleep almost at once, then woke up a couple of hours later, too hot in the sleeping-bag in the small cabin. Alex was asleep, his back to her. Carefully Ginny unzipped her bag and pushed it off her, welcoming the coolness on her skin, sticky with heat. She heard a sound in the galley and then the noise of running water. The thought of cold water made her feel thirsty. For a while she lay still, but at last thirst drove her to climb carefully over Alex and go out to the galley. Jeff was there, crushing some ice to put into a wet towel.

'How's Kay?'

He grinned at her pyjamas. 'Not so good. I think the sun got to her a bit. And the wine on top of being seasick didn't do her much good either.'

'Has she been ill again?' Jeff nodded. 'I'd better go and see her.'

Going into the other cabin, Ginny found Kay awake, her face pale, and her body very hot, but not in any terrible distress. Ginny asked her how she was, and Kay managed a weak smile. 'I'll soon be fine. I'm sorry to make all this fuss.'

'Would you like me to stay with you?'

But Jeff came in and gently put the ice-pack over Kay's forehead. She gave him a look of utter gratitude and Ginny slipped from the cabin, knowing she wasn't wanted. Jeff had found someone who needed him to look after her, and, although Kay probably didn't appreciate it at the moment, falling ill was probably the best thing she'd ever done.

Back in the galley, Ginny bathed her wrists and neck in cold water, then took an iced drink from the fridge, but then hesitated and took another.

Alex was awake and lying on top of his sleeping-bag, the light on. 'Everything OK?'

'Kay isn't very well. But Jeff is taking care of her.'

He gave her a sharp look, recognising the meaning in her tone. 'Is he, now?'

'Here, I brought you a drink.' Ginny gave it to him and climbed over him again. He watched appreciatively.

'What made you think I'd be awake?'

'I'm amazed you can sleep at all in this heat.'

He sat up and they leaned against the bulkhead, drinking companionably. 'I wouldn't mind getting a boat,' Alex remarked.

She felt a thrill of pleasure at his looking into the future instead of back into the past. 'I'm surprised that you and Jeff haven't bought one before.'

'I suppose we could have done, but there didn't seem much point.' Alex grinned. 'And if he and Kay make a go of things then I definitely think he won't be doing much more sailing.'

'No. Poor Kay. I don't think she'll be well enough to sail back tomorrow.'

'Then Jeff can hire a car to take her home and we'll take the boat back ourselves.' He took her hand in his. 'Think you can crew for me?'

A great glow of happiness shot through her at the thought of being alone with him, but Ginny only smiled and said lightly, 'Aye, aye, Cap'n.'

They finished their drinks and Alex took the empty can from her. 'We'd better get some sleep, then.' He turned off the light and lay down, making no attempt to get into the sleeping-bag, and Ginny did the same. She left a respectable gap between them but after only a moment Alex reached out and put his arms round her, drawing her towards him and holding her in the shelter of his body. He kissed her lightly on the shoulder and for a few minutes she scarcely dared to breathe in case he took things further, but he remained still and together they fell asleep again.

The sound of a boat's engine, starting up nearby, woke them the next morning. Ginny turned over, still sleepy, but came fully awake when she realised that Alex's arm lay across her. He stirred, opened his eyes and saw her. 'Hello, darling,' he murmured, and leaned forward to kiss her. Then suddenly froze, his eyes opening wide with shock.

He flinched back and Ginny saw his jaw tighten. For a brief few seconds, still half asleep, he had thought she was Venetia. Ginny dug her nails into her palms and sat up, saying briskly, 'I bags the bathroom first. I wonder how Kay is this morning? Can you move out of the way so I can get past?'

Grabbing up her toilet-bag and some clothes, Ginny left him alone in the cabin, giving him some time to recover. When she was dressed she peeped into Kay's cabin and wasn't surprised to see Jeff lying on the spare bunk; both of them were asleep. Going into the galley, she quietly began to prepare breakfast.

Alex joined her a quarter of an hour later. 'The others?'

'Still asleep. I've made you scrambled eggs on toast; that OK?'

'Mmm. Fine.'

They sat down at the table and began to eat, the percolator of coffee safely on the table between them here on the river where there was hardly any movement of the water.

'What about the tides and things? Do we have to leave at a certain time?' Ginny asked, still being brisk.

Alex glanced at his watch. 'We're all right for an hour or so.'

They were just finishing breakfast when Jeff came into the galley. He looked tired and he hadn't yet shaved. 'I smelt the coffee,' he informed them, his nose twitching like a rumpled, hungry rabbit's.

'I'll get you some,' Ginny offered. 'I expect Kay could use a cup, too.' She glanced at Jeff. 'You're not going to take her home on the boat, are you?'

He shook his head. 'Not if I can avoid it. I'll try and hire a car or get a taxi. It might be difficult on a Sunday, though.'

Alex stood up, his head lowered to avoid the ceiling. 'I'll go ashore and see if something can be arranged.'

Anyone else might have found it difficult, but Alex was back quite quickly and had fixed up for the wife of another boat owner to drive Jeff and Kay back to Bristol so long as they were ready to go in half an hour. It meant a hurried breakfast for them and they were soon gone, leaving Ginny and Alex with a slight feeling of flatness, but this soon disappeared as they made the boat ready for sea. It was another gorgeous day, so hot that after an hour or so Ginny went below and changed into her swimsuit. Alex had already stripped down to his shorts and stood, lean and bronzed, at the wheel.

He smiled when he saw her and held out a hand towards her. Ginny went to him and he put his arm round her. His voice warm, he said, 'Hello, Ginny,' and kissed her. And suddenly everything was fine again. Especially when he said, 'You're so very lovely.'

The rest of that journey back was idyllic, a day Ginny would never forget. Alex was so obviously happy, often teasing her when she got the ropes mixed up, but hugging and kissing her a lot, too. He let her take the wheel and stood behind her, his hand resting negligently on her shoulder, his almost naked body hot against hers, the breeze on their faces. They had to tack a lot of the way so it took them longer on the homeward journey and it was already evening when they regretfully took down the sails and motored back to the mooring in the marina.

Unloading the boat and leaving it clean and tidy took them another hour or more, so that it was dark and quite late when they finally drove into Bath. All the fresh air and the lack of sleep the night before had made them both tired. Alex yawned as they waited for some traffic-lights to change, and Ginny said impulsively, 'Do you *have* to get back tonight? If you like, you could stay at my place rather than drive when you're tired.'

Alex stifled another yawn and then laughed. 'That sounds a very attractive idea.'

His ready acceptance pleased and excited her; she didn't care if they spent another night as they had the last, or if he slept in the spare room; that he would be close was all that mattered.

They drew up outside the house and Ginny reached into the back to get her tote-bag, but Alex said, 'There's a light on in the sitting-room. You must have left it on yesterday morning.'

Ginny looked at the house with a puzzled frown. 'But I don't remember going in that room yesterday.'

They looked at each other and Alex got quickly out of the car. 'Stay here.'

But Ginny was right behind him as he inserted the key in the lock, pushed open the door and strode into the sitting-room.

There was a man there, but he hardly looked like a burglar. He was sitting in the armchair with a drink on the table beside him, his feet up on a stool and the television on. As they burst in he gave them a casual glance. 'Hello, Ginny.'

'Simon!'

CHAPTER SEVEN

'WHAT—what are you doing here?' Ginny demanded in astonishment. Beside her she felt Alex stiffen and her heart sank when she saw the look of cool distaste on his face. Afraid that he might just turn and leave, she put a restraining hand on his arm.

Simon had begun to grin, but he saw her action and his expression changed. 'I was over this way, so I thought I'd beg a bed for the night from you.' He glanced from her to Alex. 'But perhaps I'd be in the way.'

'Not at all,' Alex said stiffly.

Inwardly furious, Ginny said, 'Simon, I don't think you've met my brother-in-law, Alex Warwick.'

'Ah, so you were Venetia's husband.' Simon raised a hand in a casual gesture of greeting but didn't attempt to stand. His eyes went over Alex assessingly, and Ginny could almost hear his brain working. So this is the man my wife was really in love with, the man she had to leave behind in England and promise never to see again.

'How did you get in here?' she asked, wanting Alex to know that she hadn't given Simon a key.

'I remembered your speaking about your neighbour, so I knocked on her door and she let me in.'

'She just let you in?'

'Well, I did mention that I was your husband,' Simon said smoothly, enjoying himself.

'Oh, thanks a million!' Ginny's hand was still on Alex's arm, but she had felt his inner withdrawal. She could make a pretty accurate guess at his thoughts, too, but she wasn't about to let him just walk away again. 'Why didn't you phone and let me know you were coming?'

'I tried to, but all I got was the damned answerphone.' Simon gave her a plaintive look but there was devilment deep in his eyes. 'Anyone would think you aren't pleased to see me.'

Ginny tried to pull herself together; she mustn't let him upset her. Letting go of Alex's arm, she walked further into the room. 'You're always welcome, you know that,' she said lightly. 'You couldn't reach me because I've been away for the weekend.' Adding rather sardonically as she looked at Simon, 'Alex and I went on a boat trip with some friends.' She put her hand on the back of a chair, gripping it. 'How about pouring us a drink? What would you like, Alex?'

But he shook his head. 'I've left the car open. I'll get your bag.'

He went out and Simon stood up, came over to her and kissed her. 'Am I *de trop*?'

'A bit,' Ginny admitted.

'Sorry.' He put a comforting hand on her shoulder, but removed it as Alex came in with her bag. 'Let me get you a drink, Alex. What would you like?'

'Thanks, but I'm driving.' He glanced at Ginny, and she felt a wave of despair, knowing that their earlier closeness was lost. 'You two must have a lot to talk about so I'll push off. Goodnight, Ginny. See you.'

He gave Simon a brief nod and went out of the door, but Ginny ran after him. Outside on the pavement, she caught him up and pulled him round to face her. 'I didn't invite him here, Alex. And nothing has changed. I certainly haven't. I'm still the same person as I was this afternoon.'

'I know that,' he answered roughly.

'So why are you treating me as if I've suddenly become a stranger? Someone you don't even like?'

His jaw tightened, but then Alex sighed and said, 'I suppose while he was only a name it was easy not to think about him, but seeing the man who was your husband, picturing you with him—it's not so easy to ignore.'

Ginny gave him an incredulous look. 'Good heavens! I think you're jealous.'

Alex looked equally startled. 'Of course I'm not jealous,' he said shortly.

'Then why are you rushing away?' She had almost said running away.

A flash of anger came into his eyes. 'I'm not. You hardly want me there while you discuss old times.'

She gave him a brilliant smile. 'You *are* jealous. Oh, good!'

Alex stared at her, torn between emotions, but then his sense of humour won and he laughed. 'All right, maybe I am a little.' Putting a hand on her arm, he suddenly pulled her to him and kissed her hard on the mouth. 'He was too damn old for you.' Then he got in his car and drove quickly away.

Her spirits soaring, Ginny stood on the pavement and watched until he was out of sight, hugging to herself the knowledge that she had the power to charm him. She felt as if she had passed some kind of test with flying colours and that her life would always be that much better because of it.

'Are you going to stand there all night?' Simon's voice from the doorway brought her back to reality. She laughed and ran to join him.

She had already guessed that Simon hadn't just happened to be in the area; he was the sort of person who always made sure that he had a good hotel to stay in if necessary. So when they got back in the sitting-room she said, 'OK, what's the real reason for coming here?'

He grinned in pleasure. 'Ah, the perspicacity and directness of an ex-wife.'

'Is this going to take a while?'

'It may,' he admitted.

'Then I think I'll get myself a drink first.' Ginny poured herself a long, non-alcoholic drink and refreshed Simon's glass before settling herself on the sofa, her feet curled under her. 'OK. Go ahead.'

'If you're quite sure you're comfortable...'

She laughed, remembering that it was his dry sense of humour that she had always found attractive. 'Get on with it, Simon. I take it you're having wife trouble?'

'Yes, but not quite how you think. Janet is getting a divorce.'

Ginny looked at him in real surprise; Janet was his first wife and the mother of his children, although they were almost grown now. 'Good heavens, I thought she was perfectly happy.'

'Apparently not. She has upped and left, with bag, baggage and furniture, swearing that she'll never go back.' Despite the flippancy there was a note of satisfaction in his voice that he couldn't hide.

Ginny gave him a shrewd look. 'And you wouldn't at all mind having the bag, baggage, and even the furniture move in with you.'

He nodded. 'You were right when you told me I should never have left her. But there's one problem.'

'Wife number four? Sonia?'

'Ye-e-s, and also the fact that there was a number two and a number three.'

'Well, Janet has a point. What are you going to do?'

For perhaps the first time in his life Simon looked uncertain. 'I don't know. I'm afraid of frightening her off and yet I'm equally afraid that if I do nothing she might find someone else, or even change her mind and go back home. But I want her to know that— well, that I still care.'

'Quite a problem,' Ginny commented.

He nodded. 'So I thought I'd come and see you, use you as a sounding board. Because you're in the same delicate kind of position, aren't you?'

Thinking about it, Ginny supposed she was in a way. Pensively, she said, 'You have to tread carefully. You can't just rush in. But if you do tell Janet that you care then you must make sure she knows it's for keeps this time. You must assure her that there won't be any more playing around.' She looked at him and smiled. 'It might even be a good idea to convince her that you're getting over the hill a bit, that your roving days are over.' Simon pulled a face at her and she laughed. 'And I definitely shouldn't tell her that you spent a night here with me.'

'No,' he agreed. 'Although it might not be a bad thing if Sonia somehow found out.'

'Oh, no, you don't,' Ginny said sharply, sitting up straight. 'And if you came here with that in mind you can leave now. My own—future isn't secure enough for you to use me in a divorce case.'

'Simmer down, I won't.' He gave her a shrewd look. 'Alex wasn't at all pleased to see me.'

'Not a lot of men are,' Ginny said tartly, but relented and said, 'I told you, it's like walking on eggshells; sometimes they break and stick in your feet.'

'And are your feet metaphorically covered in eggshells because of me?'

Ginny gave a small sigh. 'They were, but I think it will be all right.'

'I'll go, if you like.'

'No.' Ginny shook her head decisively. 'Alex knows that we're still friends. He'll just have to accept that.'

'Good for you. I don't feel like having to find somewhere else to stay at this time of night.'

They talked for quite a long time, discussing Simon's marital problems; or at least Ginny listened while Simon talked. It had been one of the closest areas of their marriage, her ability to listen while he talked out problems, occasionally asking a question or raising an idea that often helped him. It was the early hours of the morning before Ginny protested that she couldn't keep her eyes open another minute. 'We'll talk again in the morning, OK?'

Simon shook his head. 'No need, I know what I have to do now.'

Ginny smiled at him. 'You knew all along—you just needed to convince yourself that you have the courage to do it.' She got to her feet. 'I'll make up a bed for you.'

Simon, too, got to his feet and slipped a familiar arm round her waist. 'Is that necessary? Couldn't we—for old times' sake...?' He left the suggestion hanging in the air.

'Certainly not,' Ginny answered firmly. 'You're in enough trouble as it is.'

He sighed. 'I suppose you're right. But it's a great shame, because you're looking very delectable.'

She laughed at him and pushed him away. 'Go to bed, Simon.'

He left around nine the next morning to drive back to London. Ginny saw him off and noticed a few curtains twitching, Clare's among them. In no time at all, she guessed, everyone in the street would know that she had been married. Probably Clare thought she still was; trust Simon not to mention that they had divorced nearly two years ago. Going back into the house, Ginny got down to all the Monday morning jobs, waiting for two things to happen. The first, that Clare would soon be round, she was quite sure of; the second, that Alex would phone, she was less certain about.

She didn't have long to wait for Clare, who was knocking on the door by ten o'clock. Ginny told her, quite frankly, who Simon was, and Clare went home an hour later happy in the knowledge that she had some gossip to spread. The longed-for phone call from Alex didn't come until the evening, but Ginny's heart lifted immeasurably when she heard his voice.

'Has he gone?'

'Yes, of course.'

'What did he want?' So Alex, too, had seen through Simon's excuse.

Briefly, Ginny explained. 'Have you heard how Kay is?' she asked, dismissing Simon from their lives.

'She's fine again now, evidently. It's just that she's a terrible sailor.'

'She did marvellously to hold out for even a day.'

'So Jeff seems to think. He seems to be really hooked this time.'

'Good. I'm glad.'

'What have you been doing today?'

'Stripping down the spare bed that Simon slept in.'

'Were you, indeed?'

'I thought you might like to know that.'

Alex chuckled. 'Why don't you come over here and I'll take you out to dinner?'

Ginny gave an inward sigh of happiness. 'I'm on my way.'

The next few weeks were the happiest of Ginny's life. She saw Alex two or three times a week, except when she was away working. Sometimes they made up a four with Jeff and Kay, but more often they went out alone. It was a period of high summer, an idyllic time for their relationship to grow. They took it slowly, unhurriedly, setting their pace to the long, hot summer days. It was a time of discovery for them both; a time for Ginny to be sure that she liked Alex as well as loved him. And for Alex there was time to see her as an individual and not just as the clone of the woman he had loved and lost. There were still infrequent occasions, though, when he forgot and went to call her Venetia, which brought the tension back for a while, but these became fewer as the weeks passed.

After the university broke up for the summer vacation Alex had to attend a conference in Milan, where he was to read a paper. 'I wish now that I hadn't promised to go,' he complained.

They were in his rooms at the university, the night before he was to leave, sitting on a leather settee, Ginny leaning on the arm with her legs across his lap. They had been out to dinner and she felt warm and content. 'It's only for a week,' she pointed out.

'Yes, but I'll hardly have got back before you're off to America.'

'It's something I can't get out of, I'm afraid. It's a fashion show being put on by a designer I owe a lot to. He helped me a great deal when I first arrived in New York, and I can't let him down.'

Alex's arm tightened round her waist. 'I'm half afraid that you'll be lured into staying in America. Do you promise to come back?'

'You know I will.'

He kissed her, his mouth insinuating, his hand on her breast. To feel his lips on hers, his tongue gently exploring her mouth, to have his fingers touch her skin, knowledgeably arousing her, were sensations so erotic that Ginny had to dig her nails in his shoulders to stop from crying out. Her breath grew short, panting, her body arching beneath his hands. They hadn't yet made love, but with every passing day they both knew that the time was coming nearer.

'You're so exquisite,' Alex murmured against her throat. He unbuttoned her shirt, parted it, and bent to kiss her breasts. This time Ginny did moan, her hands in his hair, but then there was a sharp knock on the door and Alex sat up. 'Damn!'

He pushed back his hair and stood up while Ginny hastily rebuttoned her shirt.

'OK?'

She nodded, and he opened the door. It was Jeff and Kay. They had their arms round each other's waists and such big smiles on their faces that it was obvious they were bursting with news.

'Sorry to butt in,' Jeff said. 'But we thought you'd like to know. We've just got engaged.'

'Why that's marvellous!' Alex drew them into the room. 'I couldn't be more pleased.' He kissed Kay and pumped Jeff's hand. 'Congratulations.'

Ginny added her own pleased good wishes, and Alex unearthed a bottle of champagne from a cupboard, saying, 'I've had this put by for exactly this occasion for the last ten years. It should be pretty potent by now.'

They drank to the health and happiness of the engaged couple, Alex without a tremor in his voice as he made the toast.

'What are your plans?' Ginny wanted to know. 'When is the wedding?'

'We've hardly had time to think of that,' Kay protested. 'All this only happened today.'

'But I've persuaded her to come on the dig in Italy with me,' Jeff interrupted.

The grin was still on his face, looked as if it was going to be permanently attached there from now on, and Ginny felt very happy for him. She felt excited, too, sharing Jeff's and Kay's feeling that they were at the start of something wonderful. But when she glanced at Alex she saw that, although he was smiling, there was an inner part of him that had withdrawn from the celebration. Instinctively she knew that he was thinking about Venetia, remembering his own hopes for the future when they had got engaged. He felt her eyes on him and his brows flickered. Deliberately he made an effort and dragged himself back to the present. He winked at her and Ginny smiled back, but couldn't keep the sad look of wistful longing from her eyes.

Jeff and Kay were on such a high that they stayed, sitting hand in hand on the settee, talking, formulating plans for the future, until late.

'You will be my best man, won't you?' Jeff asked Alex. 'After all, I went through it for you.'

Alex burst into laughter. 'How could I possibly refuse such a beautifully worded invitation?'

Kay looked at Ginny. 'I'd love to ask you to be my bridesmaid,' she said doubtfully, 'but ...'

'But if you've any sense you won't,' Ginny finished for her. 'I'm much too tall. You need some sweet little girls in Victorian dresses and pantaloons.'

Kay's face lit. 'That sounds lovely. Do you think you could help me design my dress?'

'Of course.'

The two girls began to talk dress styles, much to the men's amusement, until Alex stood up and said, 'If you lot don't mind, I have a plane I have to catch at some primitive hour in the morning, so I'm going to turn you out.'

The others said goodnight and went off together to Jeff's rooms, while Alex walked Ginny down to her car.

'Have a good trip to Milan,' she said.

'Mm.' He seemed a little preoccupied. 'Ginny?' He put his hands on her arms.

'Yes?'

But he hesitated, and then shook his head. 'See you when I get back. Sure you're OK to drive?'

'Yes, fine. Goodnight, Alex.'

He kissed her lightly, but suddenly pulled her roughly against him and kissed her hard on the mouth, a fiercely masculine kiss that let her know who was boss.

'Wow!' She gave him a surprised look, but then he had opened the car door and she got in, waving as she drove away.

Alex called her from Milan a couple of times, but Ginny spent a very frustrated week waiting for him to come home. Sometimes she wanted him so badly that it was like a real, physical ache, and she grew restless, unable to settle to anything until she'd played a long game of tennis or taken some other exercise. She'd joined a tennis club, went swimming at least twice a week, and had taken up jogging again. But although it did wonders for her figure it didn't do much to ease the sexual hunger. She respected Alex's need to take things slowly, but she was a healthy girl who was very much in love, and sometimes it was hard, especially when she knew just how virile and passionate Alex could be.

Her comfort was that Alex was so much happier now. The occasions on which he seemed to withdraw into his own thoughts, his memories and grief, were becoming fewer, at least when she was with him. But he had never taken her to meet his family or gone with her when Ginny had visited her mother, although she'd asked him if he wanted to. She thought she could guess why: he didn't want his family to think the obvious—that he was only going out with her to try to recreate Venetia. She respected him for that, but realised that until he was ready to take her to meet his family he was still unconvinced himself.

One day while Alex was away Ginny invited Kay to dinner. They talked weddings and looked at designs for dresses. Kay was so happy that she wanted to share it and said impulsively, 'Maybe you and Alex will be preparing for your own wedding soon. You must have a white wedding; you'll look so beautiful in a wedding dress,' Kay said generously.

Ginny smiled. 'Maybe we'll get round to marrying one day, but I don't think it will be for quite some time yet.'

'Because Alex is a widower? But you're made for each other.'

Ginny gave her a quick, wistful look. 'Do you think so?'

'Of course. Doesn't everyone?' Kay laughed. 'And it will be all right for me to be your bridesmaid, because I'm so much smaller.'

'I've an idea that if Alex and I ever get married it will be a quickie in a register office. It would be nice to have a white wedding next time, though,' she murmured dreamily, gazing into space.

'Next time?' Kay stared at her. 'Do you mean that—that you've been married before?'

Ginny looked at her and realised that if Kay was going to be a permanent friend it was time to put her in the picture. 'Yes, I'm divorced. And I don't think

you know that Alex was married to my twin sister—
my identical twin. That's why there are—problems.'

It seemed so strange to say it baldly like that,
summing up the whole situation in a couple of sen-
tences. Somehow it all seemed rather trivial when all
the emotions were put into plain words. She didn't
explain further, and Kay was too well-bred to ask, but
from it Ginny found a new kind of determination.
She decided that she would give Alex until Christmas
and if their relationship wasn't resolved by then she
would have to ask him to make up his mind. Perhaps
that was what he was waiting for, she thought wor-
riedly. Perhaps he couldn't bring himself to betray
Venetia's memory.

Alex drove himself back from the airport, but he
phoned Ginny the same afternoon, almost as soon as
he got back, and asked if he could come over.

'Yes, of course. Will we be going out?'

'How about taking a walk in the country?'

'Sounds great. See you soon, then.'

By the time Ginny had showered, put on a cotton
skirt and sun-top, clipped back her hair and found a
pair of suitable sandals, Alex was at the door. She
ran down to greet him, her eyes going to his face, and
he took her hands in his, holding them tightly before
he kissed her. He drove to Avebury and took her hand
as they walked round the great circle of standing
stones, a primitive place of worship built by ancient
man. Long shadows lay across the grass, the sun a
great glow low in the sky, and they had the place to
themselves.

For a while they walked in silence, but it became a
tense one, both of them aware that Alex had some-

thing on his mind. 'I've been doing a lot of thinking while I was away,' he said eventually, his voice abrupt even though he had been silent for so long. 'Seeing Jeff and Kay so happy, being away from you and missing you, it made me realise just how much I need you, Ginny.'

'Need me?' She came to a stop and turned to face him.

'Yes.' He put his hands on her waist, looking intently into her face. 'I want you to marry me, Ginny.'

Her throat felt suddenly tight, and she had to swallow hard to speak. But she mustn't give way to happiness yet, not quite yet. 'Why, Alex?' she managed. 'Why do you want to marry me?'

It wasn't the answer he'd expected and he gave a small frown. 'For companionship, so that we can spend the rest of our——' He stopped, his jaw tightening. 'So that we can be together. For all the reasons that people get married, I suppose.'

She looked at him, waiting, but he didn't say the words she wanted to hear. 'You say you missed me; is that why you need me, because you were lonely, because you don't want to be alone again?'

'That's part of it, yes.'

'Part of it?' She asked the question with difficulty, trying not to get emotional. 'Is the other part that I look like Venetia?' She swung away from him, putting her hands up to her face.

'No! Surely you know better than that by now?' He caught her hands and pulled them down. 'I want to marry you because I need you and love you.'

'Love? *Me?* You're sure?'

'Of course.' He gave her a little shake. 'Oh, Ginny, surely you know by now that I've always loved you—right from the beginning? From the first day we met.'

She stared at him. 'On the plane?'

He nodded. 'That's why I used to get so angry with you, tried so hard to cut you out of our lives, because I could never completely get you out of my mind, no matter how hard I tried.' He smiled at her, his eyes crinkling in the way she loved. 'So, will you marry me, my darling?'

It was what she had always wanted, always longed for during the long years, but somehow, despite his reassurance, she still felt that she couldn't say yes without reservation. She shook her head doubtfully. 'I don't know, Alex. I've an idea that if you really wanted this you wouldn't have hesitated, you wouldn't have had to go away and think about it. That isn't like you. You're usually so certain of what you want. I hope you're not doing this because you think it's what I want, and you owe it to me or something.'

'I want it more than anything in the world,' he assured her. 'But you must understand that it's taken me a while to—to come to terms with everything. It would have done with any woman, but with your being Venetia's sister, and given the feelings that I already had about you...' He spread his hands expressively.

'But are you sure that you *have* come to terms with it? We—we haven't been to bed together yet,' Ginny pointed out painfully.

Alex grinned. 'That can be remedied.' But then he grew serious again. 'My dear Ginny, you've been very patient, very tolerant, and I shall always be grateful for that. But now I think the time is right for us to get married—or at least engaged.'

'And will you take me to meet your family?'

He didn't hesitate. 'Of course.'

'They might be against our marrying.'

His eyebrows rose. 'Then they'll just have to get used to the idea,' he said shortly.

Ginny liked that. She gave a little laugh. 'I've an idea you'd better warn them first; do they know I exist?'

'Yes, of course.' But he nodded. 'You're right, it would be a good idea to tell them first.'

Neither of them mentioned ghosts, but it was strong in their minds.

'So is the answer yes? Will you marry me, Ginny?'

Walking a little away from him, Ginny put her hand on one of the ancient stones, feeling the lichen rough under her hand. She hesitated for several minutes, trying to think. Somehow this proposal had come at the wrong time or for the wrong reasons. She could feel no joy in it, it was too cold-blooded. Turning to face him, she said, 'You've had time to think about this, Alex; now I want some time. I'll give you my answer when I come back from America.'

'Not till then?'

'No, Alex. I'm sorry. I don't want to go into another marriage that I'm not absolutely sure about.'

'That's fair enough, of course.' But his voice was heavy with disappointment.

Quickly she tucked her arm into his. 'Tell me about the conference.'

There was less than a week before Ginny went to New York, and although they saw each other several times they didn't make love. There was the feeling between them that they had reached a barrier that had to be surmounted first. And yet if Alex had suddenly carried her upstairs and made love to her Ginny knew that it would have taken away all doubts. But he didn't, and because he didn't she knew that he wasn't a hundred per cent convinced.

The show in New York went well, and she attended to some business at the same time, arranging to let her flat and a house on the beach in California that she owned. She also made some guest appearances on television, looked up friends, and was reassured that her career was always here to pick up again if she needed it.

She had left England in a heatwave, found another in New York, and flew back to England in lightweight clothes only to find it pouring with rain and the summer seemingly over. By the time she walked through Customs and found Alex waiting for her she was already shivering.

'Here, put this on.' He took off his mac and put it round her shoulders, kissing her at the same time. He glanced at her trolley, piled high with luggage. 'Good grief!'

'I brought a few things back with me,' Ginny explained.

'No wonder the plane was late.'

He grinned at her and Ginny smiled back, so happy to be with him again. Taking the trolley from her, he pushed it along, Ginny clinging to his arm and telling him all about her trip. She went on telling him in the car, but he only half listened, concentrating on his driving as the day darkened and the rain teemed down, the windscreen wipers swishing back and forth at the fastest speed to keep it clear.

'How long has it been raining?'

'Only today. It's made the roads hell to drive on.'

And, to prove his point, only a few minutes later, on the outskirts of Bath, they came upon a bad accident, one car over on its roof, another bent like a concertina against a wall. A policeman was directing the slowly moving traffic past the scene, and Ginny looked past Alex to see figures lying on the roadside, one with someone's mac pulled right over it. Once past, Alex drove quickly, but they had only gone a short way when he pulled up at the side of the road. Turning to him, Ginny saw that his face was taut and grey, his whole body shaking.

'Alex!' Taking off her safety strap, she threw her arms round him in concern. 'What is it?'

'Sorry.' He tried desperately to control himself. 'It was seeing the accident. It brought it all back. Venetia.'

'Oh, no!' She tried to comfort him, but it was useless. He couldn't stop trembling. Deciding that the est thing to do would be to get him away from there, Ginny made him change places with her and drove the rest of the way home. At the house she took him inside and gave him brandy in a strong black coffee, not knowing what to do for the best, feeling helpless.

The brandy helped a little, but he sat in the chair, his hands gripping the arms, his face grey. 'Sorry about this. I haven't seen another accident since— since Venetia died.'

Ginny frowned. 'Do you mean that you actually *saw* Venetia's accident happen?' she asked in an appalled voice.

But Alex shook his head. 'Not happen, no. But I saw the—the aftermath.' He hesitated a moment but then began to speak, saying the words in a low, broken voice, as if each one was painful. Ginny almost raised a hand to stop him, but realised in time that this was something he had never spoken of before but had to now. 'We'd been taking part in an indoor tennis match for the university. It was in the evening and I'd gone there straight from work, of course, but Venetia had driven over in her own car. So we each drove home separately afterwards. It was raining, just like tonight; a heavy, sudden spring shower after a period of good weather.

'I was leading the way and got home first, but when Venetia didn't arrive after ten minutes or so I began to get worried that she might have broken down, so I went back to look for her.' He paused, his hands gripping the chair arms tightly, his eyes staring into the past, dark in his ashen face. 'When I got there the police and firemen had already arrived. They tried to keep me away, but I pushed them aside and went to her. She was trapped in the car and they were trying to get her out. She was conscious at first. She opened her eyes and knew that I was there, holding her. But then they gave her something to put her out and she didn't really wake again until a couple of days later, in the hospital.' His voice grew hoarse, ragged. 'By then we knew that she was going to die—and I think she knew it, too. She tried to fight, but she didn't have the strength. She so wanted to live. She spoke to me, my poor darling, and she said your name. She—she tried to smile at me . . .'

'Oh, don't!' Ginny ran to him, unable to bear any more herself or to see his pain. She put her arms round him, holding him, trying to comfort him, stroking his hair, murmuring his name. 'Oh, my poor Alex. Poor Alex.'

He gave a great shudder and put his hands up to his face, holding them there for several minutes before reaching out and catching Ginny's wrist. She could feel his hand still trembling but he gazed intently into her face, holding her eyes. 'Ginny,' he said hoarsely. 'I need you.'

She understood at once. It wasn't the way she had wanted it, but she loved him so much that she would give herself to him gladly. Straightening up, she took his hand. 'Come, then.' And she led him upstairs.

CHAPTER EIGHT

THE rain still drummed against the window. Ginny turned on the bedside lamp and went quickly over to close the curtains, shutting out the storm. Alex stood in the doorway for a moment, watching her, then he came in and closed the door. Ginny expected him to come to her, take her in his arms, but when he didn't she reached up to the buttons of her blouse and began to take off her clothes.

She let them fall to the floor, a pool of cotton and silk around her feet, her figure willowy and graceful, very slender except for the womanly swell of her breasts. Still Alex didn't move. His face in the lamp-light looked drawn, almost gaunt, his eyes dark and intense. Slowly Ginny walked across to him, put her hands on either side of his face and kissed him, lingeringly. He gave a great sigh and his body shook, but he didn't touch her. 'Get into bed,' he said thickly.

Troubled, she looked into his eyes, but he glanced away. After a moment, Ginny obeyed him and went over to the bed. The sheets felt cold as she got in, making her shiver. She tried not to tell herself that it all felt wrong; that at this moment they should both have been so hot with passion that she wouldn't even have noticed the sheets. But she could understand why Alex wanted her now; seeing the accident had made him realise all over again how vulnerable life was. He needed the reassurance of being close to someone, the experience of sexual fulfilment to convince himself that life could go on.

She didn't look at him while he undressed, but she heard him moving around and it was a few minutes before he joined her. Ginny turned to him, and found that he was shaking again. 'It's all right.' She went to him, moving close, her body touching the length of his.

He gave a great groan and put his hand on her waist, his fingers gripping so hard that they hurt her. 'Dear God! It's been so long, so long.'

She kissed him and he groaned again, then suddenly began to respond feverishly, pushing her back against the pillows. Ginny gave a gasp of relief and happiness, her arms going round him, holding him close, her body already beginning to yearn for his. 'Alex! Oh, Alex, I love you so much.'

There was a sweat of desire on his body now, and his breath was ragged, panting, the hand he raised to explore her hot and trembling. His mouth left hers to rain kisses on her eyes, her throat, making Ginny moan with pleasure and anticipation. Her body felt like a deep inferno of desire, craving love, a powder-keg of suppressed sexuality to which he had put the match. Desire overcame her and Ginny kissed him fiercely, her body arching towards him in desperate yearning. 'I want you,' she cried out. 'I've waited so long!'

Alex lifted himself on to his elbow and she expected him to move over her, but he said in a hoarse, rasping voice, 'For God's sake, turn off the light.'

She grew suddenly still, her thudding heart freezing in mid-beat. 'Alex?' She opened her eyes to look at him fearfully, but he gave an exclamation and jerked his arm past her to switch off the lamp.

The instant darkness felt cold, intimidating, as cold as her heart had become.

'Alex?'

He didn't answer, instead bending to kiss her again. But what spontaneity there had been had gone. Ginny tried to respond, tried to get back into her former mood, closing her eyes and fiercely telling herself it would be all right, all right. It only needed him to love her; even if he wanted it to be just slow and tender, then it would still be all right. But his kisses now were tense, almost forced, with a kind of desperation in them as he took her mouth, bruising her lips as he tried to ignite his own passion.

After a few minutes more, Alex raised his head again. 'I'm sorry, Virginia. I—I just can't.'

He'd never called her by her full name before and somehow it seemed to put a space between them. 'You had a shock tonight, it——'

'For God's sake don't say it doesn't matter,' Alex said in sudden, sharp anger.

'I was going to say it's understandable,' Ginny soothed. 'Why don't you lie back and relax for a while? There's no rush. We have all night, don't we?'

Reluctantly he lay back, but she could feel the tension in him. Lying on her side, Ginny began to talk to him softly, recalling their trip on the boat, telling him again about America, trying to take his mind away from tonight. She stroked his arm as she did so, and after a while let her hand steal to his chest and gently explore its smooth planes, the strong column of his neck and the breadth of his shoulders. Gradually she felt the tension ease, the tight knots in his neck relax. She began to kiss him then, small kisses on his shoulder and chest, not on his mouth, the while her hand began to stroke him further down on his stomach and hips.

After a while Ginny moved partly over him, letting her leg rub against his. Alex shuddered convulsively and for a wonderful moment she thought that his body had started to harden with desire, but it was the rigidity of returning tension. She knew then that it wasn't going to be any good. Alex knew it too, and sat up. 'I can't,' he said violently. 'Not in this room. Not in this bed.'

'It's just a bed. Just a room. And there's no one here but you and me, Alex.'

His jaw tightened but he shook his head. 'I'm sorry.'

'We could go to a hotel for the night,' she offered, remembering how, long ago, she had made Alex take her to a hotel because she hadn't wanted him to make love to her in Venetia's bed. History repeating itself, she thought with chagrin.

But again he shook his head. 'I don't think there would be any point. I'd better go.'

'Why don't we just go to sleep and see how things work out in the morning,' Ginny coaxed. 'You're too tense now, but tomorrow you might——'

'No!' Alex burst out. 'God, Ginny, don't sound so damned practical and patronising. I'm not a teenager.'

Anger born of wretchedness and frustration filled her. 'This was your idea, not mine.'

'I know. I'm sorry. I'll leave.' He got out of bed and began to dress.

Disappointment filling her heart, Ginny said, 'Before I went to America you asked me to marry you. Don't you want to hear what my answer is?'

Alex was shrugging himself into his shirt, but now he grew still. 'Maybe—we ought to reconsider that,' he said stiffly.

'You're darn right we ought!' Rejection making her bitterly angry, Ginny came to her knees, the sheet pulled up round her. 'Just what kind of marriage did you expect us to have, Alex? Something platonic? One in name only? A nice, gentle companionship? Well, no, sorry! I want a *man* in my bed, not a——'

'All right!' he broke in fiercely. 'I get the message. It was the wrong place and the wrong time—and maybe we're the wrong people.'

'No,' Ginny said fiercely. 'Not the wrong people. Not if you face up to being a man.'

'Face up to being a failure, you mean,' Alex said bitterly.

'No. Being a man is realising your shortcomings and conquering them. It's just that you can't make up your mind whether you want to live in the past or the present. Venetia's dead,' she said brutally. 'If you want to go on living with her ghost, then fine. But don't expect me to hang around, waiting for you to start living again; I had to make a life for myself once and I can do it again.'

'And a nice mess you made of it,' Alex sneered, pushing his shirt into his trousers.

'But at least I tried to live, I didn't just let myself wallow in self-pity.'

He glared at her, as angry as her, his own failure adding to his fury, making him want to hurt. 'It's hardly any wonder I didn't make it with someone who's obviously slept around as much as you have.'

Ginny gasped. 'You louse!' She stood up on the bed, clutching the sheet around her, and pointed at the door. 'Get out of here—and don't come back until you've made up your mind what you want.'

'My pleasure,' Alex gritted, pulling on his shoes. 'And when I do find a woman I want to make love to, *I'll* be the one to make the running!'

His parting shot echoed round the room as he ran down the stairs. Ginny heard the front door slam and the car almost immediately pull away.

She stood there, still seething with anger, but the anger suddenly died and she looked round the room, hardly able to believe that the row had happened, that Alex had gone. Slowly she crumpled down to sit cross-legged on the bed. He'll come back, she thought. He wouldn't just leave like this. When he's had time to simmer down, he'll come back. He didn't, of course, and, when she'd had time to become detached enough to think about it, Ginny realised that his pride wouldn't let him. To fail sexually must be one of the most humiliating experiences a man could go through. No matter that Alex had had everything against him, every mental block in his way; he would still feel utterly dejected. And probably afraid, too. He had said that it had been a long time, the fear must be there now that he was incapable of ever having sex again.

Ginny tried to think where it had gone wrong, and soon saw that she should either have said no, wait, or taken him to a hotel, a place where there were no memories. An impartial bed. She looked round the room, trying to see it with Alex's eyes. She had changed it as much as she could, but to him it would always be the bed he had shared with Venetia; her portrait would always hang over the fireplace and her scent linger in the air. I'll put the place up for sale tomorrow, Ginny decided. I should have done it as soon as I got here. And I'll move out, rent a flat or something.

She lay back on the pillows, wondering what was going to happen. Would Alex be so angry, so humiliated, that he never came back? Maybe it would be better if he didn't. Maybe they just weren't destined to be together, Ginny thought, her morale low, her feelings hopeless. The duvet had fallen on the floor and she pulled it around her, nestling into its comforting warmth. The clock told her that it was over two hours since Alex had left; maybe he might phone now that he must have got back to Bristol. But the phone didn't ring and the ticking of the clock was the only sound in the room until Ginny began to quietly cry herself to sleep.

She had unquiet dreams and woke early, surprised at first to find herself naked. Immediately unhappiness flooded back with memory and Ginny got out of bed, feeling low and lethargic, not only from last night but also from jet lag. She showered and went to dress, but only then realised that all her luggage was still in Alex's car. For a moment she was annoyed, but then felt a stab of joy. It meant he would have to bring it back and she would see him again. There might be a chance to put things right. Her spirits soaring, Ginny went back in the bathroom to wash and blow-dry her hair, then dressed in tan-coloured trousers and a cream silk shirt with a loose cardigan over the top. Make-up was difficult, as her best stuff was in one of her suitcases, but Ginny made the most of what she could find. That done, she had breakfast, expecting the phone to ring any moment, then went up to tidy her bedroom.

It was as she was making the bed that her foot kicked against something and she found Alex's wallet on the floor. Picking it up, Ginny looked at it and smiled, wondering if leaving it behind had been deliberate or subconscious. Whichever, it would definitely bring him back—and soon. Putting it in the bedside cabinet, Ginny went downstairs again, whistling to herself, her hopes rising ever higher.

Half an hour later the bell rang and she ran to answer it. It was Clare. Well, that figured. She and Alex had been yelling at each other so loudly last night that Clare had probably heard them through the wall. But it seemed that the Georgian developers had built thicker walls than she'd supposed, because Clare was only eager to know about her trip to the States. They talked for about an hour, Ginny's nerves tense, her ears straining for the sound of Alex's key turning in the lock.

Clare went away at last, but Alex still hadn't come. Ginny made herself a sandwich, but was too uptight to eat it. She roamed around the house, never far from the phone, willing Alex to get in touch, knowing that this time the first move had to come from him. But as the day wore on her despair grew. *Surely* he must see that last night was just a terrible culmination of circumstances? Now that he'd had time to think about it he must realise that it wouldn't happen again in different surroundings.

Remembering her resolution of last night, Ginny picked up the phone and called an estate agency, telling them she wanted to put the house on the market immediately. They promised to send someone round to see the house as soon as possible, and she put the phone down, comforted by the knowledge that she could tell Alex about it when he came. At four in the afternoon, the doorbell rang, and she went to open it, expecting to find the man from the estate agency, but there was a taxi outside.

'Mrs Blake?' the taxi-driver enquired.

Ginny frowned; she had never used that name in England and hardly ever in America, having used her maiden name professionally and reverting to it after her divorce. 'Yes?'

'A Mr Warwick of Bristol has sent some cases along for you.' It took him two or three trips to bring all the cases into the house for her. Ginny stood aside, saying nothing, her heart filling with anguish that Alex hadn't brought them himself. The cases all piled in the hall, the driver said, 'And Mr Warwick sent this letter for you. He said I'm to take back something.'

Slowly, her hands trembling, Ginny took the letter he held out to her. 'Just—just a minute.' Leaving the man in the hall, she went into the sitting-room and shut the door, needing the privacy to read Alex's letter. It was quite brief.

Ginny, it's obvious that things aren't going to work out for us. It was a mistake to think they ever could, and I don't see any point in our ever meeting again. Please don't blame yourself in any way; it's entirely my fault. I wish you well in whatever course you take in the future. Please return my wallet via the taxi-driver. Alex.

The abruptness of it, the lack of any form of endearment, infuriated her. He hadn't even made any real apology, just said that it was his fault. Well, it was certainly that all right, Ginny thought in intense anger. The coward! Didn't he have the courage to face her any more? Pulling open a drawer in the desk so hard that she scattered the contents on the floor, Ginny scrabbled around until she found a pen. Then she turned his note over and wrote on it, 'If you want your wallet, come and get it yourself!', stabbing the pen violently down, almost as if she were stabbing Alex, an action that would have given her a great deal of pleasure at that moment. Shoving the letter back into the envelope, she took it out to the driver.

'Take this back to Mr Warwick and make sure you give it to him personally, will you, please?'

Still seething with anger, Ginny spent the next hour or so pacing up and down, working out all the things she would say to Alex when he finally came. And when I've told him all that, she thought, then I'll—then I'll ... Her heart suddenly filled with frustrated longing. Then I'll make him get in the car with me and we'll drive to a quiet hotel somewhere, and we'll go to bed and we'll make love all night long. And this time it will be all right, it will be wonderful again. It *has* to be, because we both love each other and it just *has* to work out right next time.

It wasn't until five hours had passed that it finally sank in that Alex wasn't going to come. But even then Ginny could hardly bring herself to believe it; she sat in the chair, quite still, just waiting, until long into the night.

The man from the estate agency came soon after nine the next morning. There were dark shadows of tension and lack of sleep around Ginny's eyes, but they only served to enhance the delicate, haunting beauty of her face. He had to climb over the cases that were still piled in the hall.

'Are you moving out already?' he asked.

'Oh—no, I just got back from a trip.'

He looked round the house, measured the rooms, discussed prices and assured her of his best services, and then left. Ginny listened but wasn't really with it. She didn't even offer the poor man a cup of coffee. But when he'd gone she made the effort to take the cases upstairs and start unpacking them. Thinking that she was to be based in England from now on, Ginny had brought home all the clothes she had left behind in America. There were a great many of them, and she soon filled the section of the built-in wardrobes she had been using; the space Alex had left empty when he moved out two years ago. The largest part of the wardrobes, that Venetia had used, hadn't been touched and still contained all her dead sister's things. Now, as Ginny unpacked one of her own suitcases, she then filled it with Venetia's clothes, resolutely folding them without really looking at them. But at the far end of the wardrobe she found a dress carefully covered with a long plastic dress-bag. A white dress. Venetia's wedding dress, Ginny realised with a sudden surge of grief.

Ginny hadn't gone to her sister's wedding, of course, and had never seen a photograph of her in the dress because Alex had taken all the wedding photos away. Unable to resist, Ginny took the dress out of the wrapper and laid it on the bed. It was very beautiful. A rich, creamy-white satin with a lace over-skirt, the bodice tight-fitting and beautifully embroidered, the short sleeves like the delicate petals of a flower. The head-dress and veil were there, too, along with high-heeled satin shoes. A piece of confetti in the shape of a horseshoe fluttered to the carpet as Ginny held up the dress, and she felt a great surge of anger. Why did people have to die? Why? It was so unfair. Death was unfair.

But so was life. Ginny looked in the mirror and thought that life was damn awful, too. She held the dress in front of her, trying to imagine how Venetia would have looked in it. Would she have had her hair up or down? she wondered. Down, probably. She picked up the head-dress and veil and put them on, trying her hair both ways. But either way looked silly with a sweater and jeans. Without really thinking about it, Ginny took off her outer clothes and put on the dress, stepping into it and zipping it up at the back. Immediately she felt close to Venetia, could faintly smell the scent she had worn, could imagine the sensations she had felt when she looked at herself in the mirror. The dress fitted perfectly but was too long until she put on the shoes. Yes, Venetia would have worn her hair down. Ginny pulled the veil down over her face to see the effect.

She stood, staring at her reflection in the mirror for a long time, lost in memories, thinking of what might have been, but then sighed and turned away. But as she did so she caught a sound from downstairs. Going out on to the landing, she saw the front door open and Alex come in. He closed the door and stood irresolute for a moment, looking towards the door of the sitting-room, but perhaps she made some small sound, because he glanced up. He froze, every sense suspended in stunned disbelief, his face suddenly drained of colour, as pale as the ghost that for a nerve-shattering moment he thought she was. But then the truth hit him and he gave a great cry of anguished fury. *'Take it off!'*

He came leaping up the stairs, too fast for Ginny, who hardly had time to turn and run before his rage. He caught her just inside the bedroom and spun her round.

'Take it off! You bitch! How dare you put on her dress?'

Frightened to death, she tried to obey him but he grabbed hold of the veil and pulled it off, catching her hair as he did so and hurting her. Ginny cried out, but the pain suddenly made her gloriously, furiously angry. She hit out at him and caught him across the face. 'You coward! You get away from me.'

Alex gave a snarl of pure rage and then they were fighting, Ginny clawing at him with her nails, Alex's lips drawn back in fury as he fended her off and tried to grab hold of her. He caught one of her wrists, but she struggled wildly, yelling at him, 'I hate you! I wish I'd never met you. You're just a yellow-bellied coward who doesn't have the guts to—— Oh!' Ginny gasped, as Alex suddenly jerked her towards him and pulled her off balance.

'You little bitch! I'll teach you.' His hands went to the back of the dress, trying to undo it as Ginny struggled against him. She got a hand free and scratched his face. Alex swore and the delicate material tore in his hands. Uncaring, he began to tear the dress off her. But as the material loosened so did his hold and she stumbled, falling back across the bed. Alex fell with her and they began to fight again, rolling across the bed, yelling and cursing.

Ginny tried to bite him and Alex gave an angry exclamation. He put his hand in her hair, dragging her head away. 'Why, you . . .' He glared down at her, his mouth drawn back into a snarl—then suddenly his mouth was on hers, taking it in compulsive fury. For a moment Ginny didn't understand and tried to fight him off, but this only inflamed him further, deepening his uncontrollable hunger. And then they were rolling on the bed, not in anger but in passion. His hands tore again at the dress, then the rest of her clothes, throwing them aside in his urgency. He fumbled with his own clothes, and then he was making love to her, a savage, primitive kind of love, born out of rage, but love for all that.

Ginny gave a great cry of thankfulness and opened to him uninhibitedly. Heat spread, searing her body, and he was carried along by her mounting excitement. The thrust of his body increased, galvanised, carrying them both to the climax of desire. And as Alex reached the pinnacle of ecstasy he cried out, 'Ginny! Ginny!'

And again, when he had collapsed beside her, Alex turned to kiss her, the sweat of satiation on his skin. 'Oh, Ginny, my darling girl.'

They lay together for some time, holding each other close, their racing hearts and panting breath returning towards normal before Alex got round to taking off his clothes and Ginny pushed the shreds of the wedding dress out of sight into a cupboard.

In bed, Alex took her in his arms and gave a rich chuckle. 'I rather think I got carried away there.'

'Mmm.' Ginny nestled against him. 'Do it often, please.'

'Anything to oblige.'

She hadn't meant straight away, but obviously he had, and this time it was as wonderful as she had always remembered, gentle and tender at first but soon growing to a hungry passion that lifted them again to the heights of sensuous excitement.

Afterwards, held in the safe harbour of his arms, Ginny said dreamily, 'Thank heavens you came back. I was so afraid you wouldn't. I thought I'd lost you for ever.'

Her eyes filled with tears at the memory and Alex kissed them away. 'Hush, my darling. Everything's OK now.'

Propping herself on her elbow, Ginny looked into his face. 'You did come back for—for this, didn't you?'

Slowly Alex shook his head, a rueful smile quirking his mouth. 'No. I was just going to collect my wallet and tell you that I'd meant what I said: that we should never see each other again. God, what a fool I was.'

In a very good position to be generous, Ginny said, 'You do realise I shall have to punish you for that?'

His left eyebrow rose in fascinated expectation. 'Yeah? How?'

She smiled. 'Well, how about this for a start?'

*   *   *

They hadn't got round to closing the curtains. In the morning the sun slanted through the window across Ginny's face, waking her. The golden glow enfolded her body and her mind and she lay there for several minutes, quietly giving thanks for the miracle that had brought them together. Alex was still asleep. Ginny slipped out of bed and went to close the curtains, afraid that the sunlight would disturb him; he needed his sleep, she thought with a smile of pure contentment. Once his sexual appetite had returned Alex hadn't been able to have enough of her.

She reached to close the curtains but Alex said, 'Ginny,' and she turned to face him. He gave a long sigh. 'That's how I always remembered you; with the sun behind you. So lovely. So perfect.' He held out his hand to her. 'Come here, my love.'

It was almost noon before they went down into the sun-drenched garden. The yellow roses on the bush that Alex had planted for Venetia were full blown, had reached their peak and were ready to wilt and drop. When Ginny touched one of them the petals came away in her hand. She held them for a moment before slowly letting them fall through her fingers. Watching her, guessing her thoughts, Alex said, 'She would have been happy for us.'

Ginny smiled. 'I've an idea she arranged it all.'

He laughed and put his arm round her, kissed her on the neck until she moaned with pleasure. 'You may get tired of all this,' he warned her.

She gave him a provocative look. 'Try me.'

'Yeah?'

He playfully bent to pick her up, but Ginny slipped out of his reach. 'Hey, we have all the time in the world.'

Suddenly Alex grew tense and caught her hand, holding it tightly. 'Never say that,' he said curtly.

She understood instantly. 'All right.' She put a soothing hand to his face. 'I promise I'll never take a minute for granted.' She kissed him lingeringly, bringing his thoughts back to happiness again.

When they parted, he smiled down at her. 'I've just thought of something; *were* you going to accept my proposal of marriage?'

Ginny looked up at him, her face at last able to show the love that had lain undiminished in her heart over all the years. 'Oh, I think I just might have taken pity on you and accepted.'

Alex looked smug. 'Well, at least now I can make up to you for having lost the toss of the coin and having to give me up to Venetia.'

Ginny's heart swelled with happiness, but she decided that Alex was in danger of becoming complacent, so she tilted her head to one side, gave him a challenging look and said, 'So what makes you think I lost?'

He stared at her, his mouth falling open. 'Ginny, do you mean to say that . . .?'

She laughed. 'Wouldn't you like to know!'

YOU <u>CAN</u> AFFORD THAT HOLIDAY!

Great savings can be made when you book your next holiday – whether you want to go skiing, take a luxury cruise, or lie in the Mediterranean sun – the Holiday Club offers you the chance to receive **FREE HOLIDAY SPENDING MONEY** worth up to 10% of the cost of your holiday!

All you have to do is choose a holiday from one of the major holiday companies including Thomson, Cosmos, Horizon, Cunard, Kuoni, Jetsave and many more.

Just call us* and ask if the holiday company you wish to book with is included.

HOW MUCH SPENDING MONEY WILL I RECEIVE?

The amount you receive is based on the basic price of your holiday. Add up the total cost for all holiday-makers listed on your booking form – excluding surcharges, supplements, insurance, car hire or special excursions where these are not included in the basic cost, and after any special reductions which may be offered on the holiday – then compare the total with the price bands below:-

YOUR TOTAL BASIC HOLIDAY PRICE FOR ALL PASSENGERS	HOLIDAY SPENDING MONEY
200 449	20
450 649	30
650 849	40
850 1099	60
1100 1499	80
1500 1999	110 ...
... 8500 or more	500

Having paid the balance of your holiday 10 weeks prior to travelling, your **FREE HOLIDAY SPENDING MONEY** will be sent to you with your tickets in the form of a cheque from the Holiday Club approximately 7-10 days before departure.

We reserve the right to decline any booking at our discretion. All holidays are subject to availability and the terms and conditions of the tour operators.

HOW TO BOOK

1. CHOOSE YOUR HOLIDAY from one of the major holiday companies brochures, making a note of the flight and hotel codes.

2. PHONE IT THROUGH* with your credit card details for the deposit and insurance premium, or full payment if within 10 weeks of departure and quote P&M Ref: H&C/MBC185. Your holiday must be booked with the Holiday Club before 30.6.92 and taken before 31.12.93.

3. SEND THE BOOKING FORM from the brochure to the address above, marking the top right hand corner of the booking form with P&M Ref: H&C/MBC185.

If you prefer to book by post or wish to pay the deposit by cheque, omit stage 2 and simply mail your booking to us. We will contact you if your holiday is not available.

Send to: The Holiday Club
P O Box 155 Leicester LE1 9GZ
* Tel No. (0533) 513377
Mon – Fri 9 am – 8 pm, Sat 9 am – 4 pm
Sun and Bank Holidays 10 am – 4 pm

CONDITION OF OFFER

Most people like to take out holiday insurance to cover for loss of possessions or injury. It is a condition of the offer that Page & Moy will arrange suitable insurance for you – further details are available on request. In order to provide comprehensive cover insurance will become payable upon confirmation of your holiday.

Free Holiday Spending Money is not payable if travel on the holiday does not take place.

The Holiday Club is run by Page & Moy Ltd, Britain's largest single location travel agency and a long standing member of ABTA.

N.B. Any contractual arrangements are between yourselves and the tour operators not Mills & Boon Ltd.

ABTA 99529 Page & Moy Ltd Reg No. 1151142

WIN A LUXURY CRUISE

TO THE MEDITERRANEAN
AND BLACK SEA

Ever dreamed of lazing away the days on the open sea with all you need to enjoy yourself close at hand, and spending busy, exciting hours ashore exploring romantic old cities and ports?

Imagine gliding across calm blue waters with the sun overhead in a vast blue sky, and waking up in faraway places for breakfast, such as Lisbon with its fashionable shops, or at the famous rock of Gibraltar.

Imagine sailing through the Mediterranean and stopping at Sicily with towering Mt Etna, then arriving effortlessly in Athens with all its many treasures and finally cruising along the Bosphorus and exploring the exotic city of Istanbul.

This experience of a lifetime could be yours, all you need to do is save the red token from the back of this book and collect a blue token from any Mills & Boon Romance featuring the holiday competition in December. Complete the competition entry form and send it in together with the tokens.

Don't miss this opportunity!
Watch out for the Competition
in next month's books

Next month's Romances

Each month, you can choose from a world of variety in romance with Mills & Boon. These are the new titles to look out for next month.

THE STONE PRINCESS Robyn Donald   *AEIOU*

TWO-FACED WOMAN Roberta Leigh

DIAMOND FIRE Anne Mather

THE GOLDEN GREEK Sally Wentworth

SAFETY IN NUMBERS Sandra Field

LEADER OF THE PACK Catherine George

LOVEABLE KATIE LOVEWELL Emma Goldrick

THE TROUBLE WITH LOVE Jessica Hart

A STRANGER'S TRUST Emma Richmond

HIS WOMAN Jessica Steele

SILVER LADY Mary Lyons

RELUCTANT MISTRESS Natalie Fox

SHADOW HEART Cathy Williams

DEVON'S DESIRE Quinn Wilder

TIRED OF KISSING Annabel Murray

WIFE TO CHARLES Sophie Weston

STARSIGN

STARS IN THEIR EYES Lynn Jacobs

Available from Boots, Martins, John Menzies, W.H. Smith and other paperback stockists.

Also available from Mills and Boon Reader Service, P.O. Box 236, Thornton Road, Croydon, Surrey CR9 3RU.